the perfect show

(a jessie hunt psychological suspense—book 33)

blake pierce

Blake Pierce

Blake Pierce is the USA Today bestselling author of the RILEY PAGE mystery series, which includes seventeen books. Blake Pierce is also the author of the MACKENZIE WHITE mystery series, comprising fourteen books; of the AVERY BLACK mystery series, comprising six books; of the KERI LOCKE mystery series, comprising five books; of the MAKING OF RILEY PAIGE mystery series, comprising six books; of the KATE WISE mystery series, comprising seven books; of the CHLOE FINE psychological suspense mystery, comprising six books; of the JESSIE HUNT psychological suspense thriller series, comprising thirty-eight books (and counting); of the AU PAIR psychological suspense thriller series, comprising three books; of the ZOE PRIME mystery series, comprising six books; of the ADELE SHARP mystery series, comprising sixteen books, of the EUROPEAN VOYAGE cozy mystery series, comprising six books; of the LAURA FROST FBI suspense thriller, comprising eleven books; of the ELLA DARK FBI suspense thriller, comprising twenty-one books (and counting); of the A YEAR IN EUROPE cozy mystery series, comprising nine books, of the AVA GOLD mystery series, comprising six books; of the RACHEL GIFT mystery series, comprising fifteen books (and counting); of the VALERIE LAW mystery series, comprising nine books; of the PAIGE KING mystery series, comprising eight books; of the MAY MOORE mystery series, comprising eleven books; of the CORA SHIELDS mystery series, comprising eight books; of the NICKY LYONS mystery series, comprising eight books, of the CAMI LARK mystery series, comprising ten books; of the AMBER YOUNG mystery series, comprising eight books; of the DAISY FORTUNE mystery series, comprising five books; of the FIONA RED mystery series, comprising thirteen books (and counting); of the FAITH BOLD mystery series, comprising seventeen books (and counting); of the JULIETTE HART mystery series, comprising five books; of the MORGAN CROSS mystery series, comprising thirteen books (and counting); of the FINN WRIGHT mystery series, comprising seven books (and counting); of the SHEILA STONE suspense thriller series, comprising eight books (and counting); of the RACHEL BLACKWOOD suspense thriller series, comprising eight books (and counting); and of the new THE GOVERNESS psychological suspense thriller series, comprising five books (and counting).

An avid reader and lifelong fan of the mystery and thriller genres, Blake loves to hear from you, so please feel free to visit www.blakepierceauthor.com to learn more and stay in touch.

ISBN: 978-1-0943-8554-9

BOOKS BY BLAKE PIERCE

THE GOVERNESS PSYCHOLOGICAL SUSPENSE
ONE LAST LIE (Book #1)
ONE LAST SMILE (Book #2)
ONE LAST BREATH (Book #3)
ONE LAST GOODBYE (Book #4)
ONE LAST SECRET (Book #5)

RACHEL BLACKWOOD SUSPENSE THRILLER
NOT THIS WAY (Book #1)
NOT THIS TIME (Book #2)
NOT THIS CLOSE (Book #3)
NOT THIS ROAD (Book #4)
NOT THIS LATE (Book #5)
NOT THIS NIGHT (Book #6)
NOT THIS PLACE (Book #7)
NOT THIS SOON (Book #8)

SHEILA STONE SUSPENSE THRILLER
SILENT GIRL (Book #1)
SILENT TRAIL (Book #2)
SILENT NIGHT (Book #3)
SILENT HOUSE (Book #4)
SILENT SCREAM (Book #5)
SILENT PREY (Book #6)
SILENT RITUAL (Book #7)
SILENT PRAYER (Book #8)

FINN WRIGHT MYSTERY SERIES
WHEN YOU'RE MINE (Book #1)
WHEN YOU'RE SAFE (Book #2)
WHEN YOU'RE CLOSE (Book #3)
WHEN YOU'RE SLEEPING (Book #4)
WHEN YOU'RE SANE (Book #5)
WHEN YOU'RE SILENT (Book #6)
WHEN YOU'RE GONE (Book #7)

MORGAN CROSS MYSTERY SERIES

FOR YOU (Book #1)
FOR RAGE (Book #2)
FOR LUST (Book #3)
FOR WRATH (Book #4)
FOREVER (Book #5)
FOR US (Book #6)
FOR NOW (Book #7)
FOR ONCE (Book #8)
FOR ETERNITY (Book #9)
FORLORN (Book #10)
FOR SILENCE (Book #11)
FORBIDDEN (Book #12)
FOR FEAR (Book #13)
FORSAKEN (Book #14)

JULIETTE HART MYSTERY SERIES

NOTHING TO FEAR (Book #1)
NOTHING THERE (Book #2)
NOTHING WATCHING (Book #3)
NOTHING HIDING (Book #4)
NOTHING LEFT (Book #5)

FAITH BOLD MYSTERY SERIES

SO LONG (Book #1)
SO COLD (Book #2)
SO SCARED (Book #3)
SO NORMAL (Book #4)
SO FAR GONE (Book #5)
SO LOST (Book #6)
SO ALONE (Book #7)
SO FORGOTTEN (Book #8)
SO INSANE (Book #9)
SO SMITTEN (Book #10)
SO SIMPLE (Book #11)
SO BROKEN (Book #12)
SO CRUEL (Book #13)
SO HAUNTED (Book #14)
SO SILENT (Book #15)
SO BLEAK (Book #16)
SO HOLLOW (Book #17)

FIONA RED MYSTERY SERIES
LET HER GO (Book #1)
LET HER BE (Book #2)
LET HER HOPE (Book #3)
LET HER WISH (Book #4)
LET HER LIVE (Book #5)
LET HER RUN (Book #6)
LET HER HIDE (Book #7)
LET HER BELIEVE (Book #8)
LET HER FORGET (Book #9)
LET HER TRY (Book #10)
LET HER PLAY (Book #11)
LET HER VANISH (Book #12)
LET HER FADE (Book #13)

DAISY FORTUNE MYSTERY SERIES
NEED YOU (Book #1)
CLAIM YOU (Book #2)
CRAVE YOU (Book #3)
CHOOSE YOU (Book #4)
CHASE YOU (Book #5)

AMBER YOUNG MYSTERY SERIES
ABSENT PITY (Book #1)
ABSENT REMORSE (Book #2)
ABSENT FEELING (Book #3)
ABSENT MERCY (Book #4)
ABSENT REASON (Book #5)
ABSENT SANITY (Book #6)
ABSENT LIFE (Book #7)
ABSENT HUMANITY (Book #8)

CAMI LARK MYSTERY SERIES
JUST ME (Book #1)
JUST OUTSIDE (Book #2)
JUST RIGHT (Book #3)
JUST FORGET (Book #4)
JUST ONCE (Book #5)
JUST HIDE (Book #6)
JUST NOW (Book #7)
JUST HOPE (Book #8)

JUST LEAVE (Book #9)
JUST TONIGHT (Book #10)

NICKY LYONS MYSTERY SERIES
ALL MINE (Book #1)
ALL HIS (Book #2)
ALL HE SEES (Book #3)
ALL ALONE (Book #4)
ALL FOR ONE (Book #5)
ALL HE TAKES (Book #6)
ALL FOR ME (Book #7)
ALL IN (Book #8)

CORA SHIELDS MYSTERY SERIES
UNDONE (Book #1)
UNWANTED (Book #2)
UNHINGED (Book #3)
UNSAID (Book #4)
UNGLUED (Book #5)
UNSTABLE (Book #6)
UNKNOWN (Book #7)
UNAWARE (Book #8)

MAY MOORE SUSPENSE THRILLER
NEVER RUN (Book #1)
NEVER TELL (Book #2)
NEVER LIVE (Book #3)
NEVER HIDE (Book #4)
NEVER FORGIVE (Book #5)
NEVER AGAIN (Book #6)
NEVER LOOK BACK (Book #7)
NEVER FORGET (Book #8)
NEVER LET GO (Book #9)
NEVER PRETEND (Book #10)
NEVER HESITATE (Book #11)

PAIGE KING MYSTERY SERIES
THE GIRL HE PINED (Book #1)
THE GIRL HE CHOSE (Book #2)
THE GIRL HE TOOK (Book #3)
THE GIRL HE WISHED (Book #4)

THE GIRL HE CROWNED (Book #5)
THE GIRL HE WATCHED (Book #6)
THE GIRL HE WANTED (Book #7)
THE GIRL HE CLAIMED (Book #8)

VALERIE LAW MYSTERY SERIES
NO MERCY (Book #1)
NO PITY (Book #2)
NO FEAR (Book #3)
NO SLEEP (Book #4)
NO QUARTER (Book #5)
NO CHANCE (Book #6)
NO REFUGE (Book #7)
NO GRACE (Book #8)
NO ESCAPE (Book #9)

RACHEL GIFT MYSTERY SERIES
HER LAST WISH (Book #1)
HER LAST CHANCE (Book #2)
HER LAST HOPE (Book #3)
HER LAST FEAR (Book #4)
HER LAST CHOICE (Book #5)
HER LAST BREATH (Book #6)
HER LAST MISTAKE (Book #7)
HER LAST DESIRE (Book #8)
HER LAST REGRET (Book #9)
HER LAST HOUR (Book #10)
HER LAST SHOT (Book #11)
HER LAST PRAYER (Book #12)
HER LAST LIE (Book #13)
HER LAST WHISPER (Book #14)
HER LAST SECRET (Book #15)

AVA GOLD MYSTERY SERIES
CITY OF PREY (Book #1)
CITY OF FEAR (Book #2)
CITY OF BONES (Book #3)
CITY OF GHOSTS (Book #4)
CITY OF DEATH (Book #5)
CITY OF VICE (Book #6)

A YEAR IN EUROPE
A MURDER IN PARIS (Book #1)
DEATH IN FLORENCE (Book #2)
VENGEANCE IN VIENNA (Book #3)
A FATALITY IN SPAIN (Book #4)

ELLA DARK FBI SUSPENSE THRILLER
GIRL, ALONE (Book #1)
GIRL, TAKEN (Book #2)
GIRL, HUNTED (Book #3)
GIRL, SILENCED (Book #4)
GIRL, VANISHED (Book 5)
GIRL ERASED (Book #6)
GIRL, FORSAKEN (Book #7)
GIRL, TRAPPED (Book #8)
GIRL, EXPENDABLE (Book #9)
GIRL, ESCAPED (Book #10)
GIRL, HIS (Book #11)
GIRL, LURED (Book #12)
GIRL, MISSING (Book #13)
GIRL, UNKNOWN (Book #14)
GIRL, DECEIVED (Book #15)
GIRL, FORLORN (Book #16)
GIRL, REMADE (Book #17)
GIRL, BETRAYED (Book #18)
GIRL, BOUND (Book #19)
GIRL, REFORMED (Book #20)
GIRL, REBORN (Book #21)

LAURA FROST FBI SUSPENSE THRILLER
ALREADY GONE (Book #1)
ALREADY SEEN (Book #2)
ALREADY TRAPPED (Book #3)
ALREADY MISSING (Book #4)
ALREADY DEAD (Book #5)
ALREADY TAKEN (Book #6)
ALREADY CHOSEN (Book #7)
ALREADY LOST (Book #8)
ALREADY HIS (Book #9)
ALREADY LURED (Book #10)
ALREADY COLD (Book #11)

EUROPEAN VOYAGE COZY MYSTERY SERIES
MURDER (AND BAKLAVA) (Book #1)
DEATH (AND APPLE STRUDEL) (Book #2)
CRIME (AND LAGER) (Book #3)
MISFORTUNE (AND GOUDA) (Book #4)
CALAMITY (AND A DANISH) (Book #5)
MAYHEM (AND HERRING) (Book #6)

ADELE SHARP MYSTERY SERIES
LEFT TO DIE (Book #1)
LEFT TO RUN (Book #2)
LEFT TO HIDE (Book #3)
LEFT TO KILL (Book #4)
LEFT TO MURDER (Book #5)
LEFT TO ENVY (Book #6)
LEFT TO LAPSE (Book #7)
LEFT TO VANISH (Book #8)
LEFT TO HUNT (Book #9)
LEFT TO FEAR (Book #10)
LEFT TO PREY (Book #11)
LEFT TO LURE (Book #12)
LEFT TO CRAVE (Book #13)
LEFT TO LOATHE (Book #14)
LEFT TO HARM (Book #15)
LEFT TO RUIN (Book #16)

THE AU PAIR SERIES
ALMOST GONE (Book#1)
ALMOST LOST (Book #2)
ALMOST DEAD (Book #3)

ZOE PRIME MYSTERY SERIES
FACE OF DEATH (Book#1)
FACE OF MURDER (Book #2)
FACE OF FEAR (Book #3)
FACE OF MADNESS (Book #4)
FACE OF FURY (Book #5)
FACE OF DARKNESS (Book #6)

A JESSIE HUNT PSYCHOLOGICAL SUSPENSE SERIES

THE PERFECT WIFE (Book #1)
THE PERFECT BLOCK (Book #2)
THE PERFECT HOUSE (Book #3)
THE PERFECT SMILE (Book #4)
THE PERFECT LIE (Book #5)
THE PERFECT LOOK (Book #6)
THE PERFECT AFFAIR (Book #7)
THE PERFECT ALIBI (Book #8)
THE PERFECT NEIGHBOR (Book #9)
THE PERFECT DISGUISE (Book #10)
THE PERFECT SECRET (Book #11)
THE PERFECT FAÇADE (Book #12)
THE PERFECT IMPRESSION (Book #13)
THE PERFECT DECEIT (Book #14)
THE PERFECT MISTRESS (Book #15)
THE PERFECT IMAGE (Book #16)
THE PERFECT VEIL (Book #17)
THE PERFECT INDISCRETION (Book #18)
THE PERFECT RUMOR (Book #19)
THE PERFECT COUPLE (Book #20)
THE PERFECT MURDER (Book #21)
THE PERFECT HUSBAND (Book #22)
THE PERFECT SCANDAL (Book #23)
THE PERFECT MASK (Book #24)
THE PERFECT RUSE (Book #25)
THE PERFECT VENEER (Book #26)
THE PERFECT PEOPLE (Book #27)
THE PERFECT WITNESS (Book #28)
THE PERFECT APPEARANCE (Book #29)
THE PERFECT TRAP (Book #30)
THE PERFECT EXPRESSION (Book #31)
THE PERFECT ACCOMPLICE (Book #32)
THE PERFECT SHOW (Book #33)
THE PERFECT POISE (Book #34)
THE PERFECT CROWD (Book #35)
THE PERFECT CRIME (Book #36)
THE PERFECT PREY (Book #37)
THE PERFECT BETRAYAL (Book #38)

CHLOE FINE PSYCHOLOGICAL SUSPENSE SERIES
NEXT DOOR (Book #1)

A NEIGHBOR'S LIE (Book #2)
CUL DE SAC (Book #3)
SILENT NEIGHBOR (Book #4)
HOMECOMING (Book #5)
TINTED WINDOWS (Book #6)

KATE WISE MYSTERY SERIES
IF SHE KNEW (Book #1)
IF SHE SAW (Book #2)
IF SHE RAN (Book #3)
IF SHE HID (Book #4)
IF SHE FLED (Book #5)
IF SHE FEARED (Book #6)
IF SHE HEARD (Book #7)

THE MAKING OF RILEY PAIGE SERIES
WATCHING (Book #1)
WAITING (Book #2)
LURING (Book #3)
TAKING (Book #4)
STALKING (Book #5)
KILLING (Book #6)

RILEY PAIGE MYSTERY SERIES
ONCE GONE (Book #1)
ONCE TAKEN (Book #2)
ONCE CRAVED (Book #3)
ONCE LURED (Book #4)
ONCE HUNTED (Book #5)
ONCE PINED (Book #6)
ONCE FORSAKEN (Book #7)
ONCE COLD (Book #8)
ONCE STALKED (Book #9)
ONCE LOST (Book #10)
ONCE BURIED (Book #11)
ONCE BOUND (Book #12)
ONCE TRAPPED (Book #13)
ONCE DORMANT (Book #14)
ONCE SHUNNED (Book #15)
ONCE MISSED (Book #16)
ONCE CHOSEN (Book #17)

MACKENZIE WHITE MYSTERY SERIES
BEFORE HE KILLS (Book #1)
BEFORE HE SEES (Book #2)
BEFORE HE COVETS (Book #3)
BEFORE HE TAKES (Book #4)
BEFORE HE NEEDS (Book #5)
BEFORE HE FEELS (Book #6)
BEFORE HE SINS (Book #7)
BEFORE HE HUNTS (Book #8)
BEFORE HE PREYS (Book #9)
BEFORE HE LONGS (Book #10)
BEFORE HE LAPSES (Book #11)
BEFORE HE ENVIES (Book #12)
BEFORE HE STALKS (Book #13)
BEFORE HE HARMS (Book #14)

AVERY BLACK MYSTERY SERIES
CAUSE TO KILL (Book #1)
CAUSE TO RUN (Book #2)
CAUSE TO HIDE (Book #3)
CAUSE TO FEAR (Book #4)
CAUSE TO SAVE (Book #5)
CAUSE TO DREAD (Book #6)

KERI LOCKE MYSTERY SERIES
A TRACE OF DEATH (Book #1)
A TRACE OF MURDER (Book #2)
A TRACE OF VICE (Book #3)
A TRACE OF CRIME (Book #4)
A TRACE OF HOPE (Book #5)

PROLOGUE

Tabitha Reynolds didn't want to get out of the shower.

Even though the space heater was on and waiting for her once she opened the door and stepped onto the bathmat, it was warmer inside the cozy confines of the shower. It was late December and Tabitha's Venice, California loft was notoriously drafty. Just the thought of leaving the bathroom and returning to the open living space made her shiver. Plus, for reasons she couldn't understand, her muscles felt strangely achy, and she wanted to give them a little more time to unclench.

She knew that she shouldn't complain. After all, things were mostly going her way. Ever since the divorce two years ago, her professional life had improved dramatically. She decided to turn her love of fashion into a career and started her own blog before adding YouTube, Instagram, and TikTok channels. In less than eighteen months, she'd gained over two million followers across her various platforms. That was how she'd been able to move out of her crappy Mar Vista apartment into this spacious, if admittedly chilly, loft apartment.

Her personal life, however, had gotten a little messier. Just thinking about it made her chest tighten slightly, forcing her to inhale deeply to get in the necessary air. For a while, she wasn't even interested in dating again. And after she struck gold with her fashion commentary, she didn't feel like she could trust that any of the guys she met were sincere in their interest.

Things with her nine-year-old daughter, Samantha, were also a little iffy of late. The girl had developed a bit of an attitude in recent months, and Tabitha couldn't help but wonder if it was because of the reduction in available mother-daughter time due to work. Unlike when she was a stay-at-home mom, this fashion thing was sometimes all-consuming, and Sammy often paid the price. Tabitha's eyes were suddenly a little blurry as she tried to blink back the tears that had emerged out of nowhere.

She would have felt guilty about allowing this week's activities if it hadn't been on the books for weeks. According to the custody schedule, Sammy's father was supposed to have her next week, after Christmas and through New Year's Day. But he'd specifically requested that they change it so he could take her camping and spend Christmas Day in Yosemite. Tabitha had conceded, even though she knew that Sammy wasn't super enthused to spend her Christmas in a tent surrounded by snow *and* that she would hold on to her resentment for weeks after she returned.

Since it was out of her hands, Tabitha tried to let it go. She also tried to remember that she was entitled to some downtime. That's why this evening, her friend Marnie would be coming over for a girls' night, comprised of good white wine and a double bill of crappy romantic comedies. She looked at the clock on the wall and saw that it was 4:36 p.m. Marnie would be here in just under an hour.

What ultimately made her turn off the water wasn't any pressure to get ready in time or a sense of guilt at taking a twelve-minute shower. It was the odd feeling she was experiencing. It occurred to her that all of the strange sensations she'd been experiencing over the last few minutes hadn't gone away. In fact, they seemed to be getting worse.

Her slightly blurry had escalated to full-on fuzzy. Those achy muscles were now both stiff and weak. The tension in her chest had gotten significantly more pronounced. She found it increasingly difficult to breathe, as if her upper torso muscles were refusing her instructions to breathe in and out normally.

Even wrapping the towel around her body and stepping out of the shower was a challenge, as her arms and legs weren't responding properly. She moved over to the bathroom counter and rested her palms on it for support. She wasn't sure what was going on. She'd felt fine when she entered the bathroom, but over the course of the last fifteen minutes, it was like her body had started to shut down.

She blinked several times, trying to focus. That's when she noticed something on the counter that she'd missed before. It was a canister—what looked like an aerosol spray can, hidden behind several other cans at the very back of the counter. But it didn't have any brand markings on it. It was just a silver, metal can. She didn't remember buying anything like that or getting it as a gift.

Her thoughts turned away from the can as she realized that it was no longer just difficult to breathe, it was borderline impossible. She reached over to grab her cell phone, which was resting on the counter by the sink. She wasn't sure if this was a heart attack or what, but she felt the urgent need to call 911.

But as she extended her hand for the phone, she discovered that all her limbs now seemed to be nearly paralyzed. She couldn't maintain her balance. Her fingers brushed against the phone, knocking it to the floor, Then, without warning, her entire body careened to the left and landed with a thud. It wasn't as painful as she would have expected, mostly because everything felt increasingly numb.

As she attempted to reach out for her phone, she tried to inhale deeply but found that she could barely suck in any air at all. Fear began to grip her as she realized she might not have the ability to call for help and that if this didn't get better fast, she wouldn't be able to breathe at all.

She focused all her attention on two things: reaching her phone and getting air into her lungs. She watched her fingers grip the bathmat, trying to pull her hand closer to the phone, which was only six inches away. She ordered her lips to suck in another gulp of air to give her strength to tap the phone.

But to her horror, she realized that even they were no longer responding. She could not get any air into her body. And then, without her even understanding that it was happening, her heart stopped.

Her fingers settled on top of the phone as her world went dark forever.

CHAPTER ONE

Jessie Hunt added a hint of soy sauce to the pan, then mixed it in with the slowly caramelizing Brussels sprouts. The smell made her mouth water.

At the butcher block behind her, her husband Ryan was cutting pieces of chicken thighs into cubes that would be added to the pan momentarily. She silently admired his muscular forearms, flexing as they cut. Then, she allowed herself to admire the rest of him.

She lingered on his square jaw and the firm, two-hundred pound, six-foot tall body that strained at his dress shirt before taking special notice of the features that had first attracted her to him—his warm brown eyes, shy grin, and adorable dimples.

Just off to the side of him, the red onions and mushrooms were waiting in separate bowls, ready to be included when the time was right. Neither of them were cooks on the level of her younger half-sister, but considering that Hannah wasn't here tonight, they were doing the best they could. Jessie might even allow herself a glass of wine if they were truly satisfied with the results.

She reminded herself not to get too comfortable. Just because it was approaching 6 p.m. on a Thursday evening and Christmas was only three days off, that didn't mean that she and Ryan couldn't get a call at any minute. Considering that Ryan was the detective in charge of LAPD's Homicide Special Section, or HSS, and that Jessie was the unit's criminal profiler, it was entirely possible that their dinner could be interrupted. In fact, considering that HSS specialized in cases with high profiles or intense media scrutiny—typically involving multiple victims or serial killers, it was more likely than not to happen.

Nonetheless, Jessie hoped that they wouldn't get a call tonight. They needed a quiet evening together. So much had happened in the eight months since they'd gotten married that it often felt like they hadn't gotten a chance to catch their breath.

There were the huge events, like Jessie having brain surgery after swelling caused by multiple case-related concussions. In addition, Hannah—as well as Jessie's best friend, Kat Gentry—had nearly been killed by a professional assassin hired to snuff out the lives of those closest to Jessie. And to top it all off, a vengeful serial killer named Mark Haddonfield had tried to murder her as "punishment" for not taking him under her wing as a profiler-in-training.

As Jessie stirred the contents of the pan, she almost laughed to herself at the absurdity of it. After all, that was just the big stuff. It didn't include the fact that Hannah, for whom Jessie had served as guardian the last two years, was now in her freshman year at UC Irvine, which was fifty miles and a world away. And it didn't include the ongoing couples therapy that Jessie and Ryan were going through to deal with her residual trust issues after Ryan had held back details about a case in order to protect her. His decision had ultimately put Hannah and Kat in the cross-hairs of that assassin, a woman named Ash Pierce.

"I was going to add the mushrooms," she told Ryan, "unless you think it's too early."

"No, that's good," he said, his eyes focused intently on making the cubes of meat as symmetrical as possible. "The chicken will be ready to go in too in another minute or so."

Jessie smiled. At least they could agree on dinner prep. That was something considering their lack of harmony on other issues. One in particular, while not life-threatening, could prove life-altering. That was their ongoing disagreement about whether or not to have children. Ryan, previously married and without kids, was desperate to have them. Jessie, also once-married, had suffered through a difficult miscarriage well into her pregnancy, and was far less enthused by the prospect of trying again.

Luckily, Ryan had agreed to set the issue aside until Jessie was ready to entertain it again, which meant that the last two weeks had been blissfully free of any baby talk. Of course, that didn't mean the time had been entirely blissful. After all, it was almost exactly two weeks ago that Kat's fiancé, Mitch Connor, had been gunned down.

Even now, Jessie still had trouble processing what had happened to her friend. Kat and Mitch had been leaving a movie theater when a young man named Jimmy Platt, who was holding a gun and shouting "I am the new chosen one! I will complete the mission begun by my predecessor. I am the assassin now!" fired at Kat.

Mitch, a former Sheriff's deputy who'd just gotten a position with the LAPD, leapt in front of her, taking the bullet intended for her. A nearby cop gunned down Platt and called for an ambulance. But soon after arriving at the hospital, Mitch died.

Kat, in a frenzy of fury, assumed the shooting was at the behest of Ash Pierce. The assassin had recently emerged from a coma and was claiming to suffer from amnesia, recalling none of her prior murderous acts. Kat didn't buy it. Luckily, Jessie was able to talk Kat down before she entered Pierce's hospital room and shot her in cold blood.

As it turned out from the subsequent investigation, Jimmy Platt had actually been acting on the instructions of Mark Haddonfield, who had released a manifesto despite his imprisonment. His online screed had implored others to pick up his mantle of murder and kill both Jessie and those she loved. Platt was trying to do just that to Kat when Mitch stepped in front of her that night.

The fact that Kat had been prevented from accidentally killing the wrong psychopath didn't give her much comfort. She rarely left her apartment these days, and visits from Jessie and Ryan, among others, had meet met with ambivalence at best.

"Ready for the chicken?" Ryan asked, snapping her out of her thoughts momentarily.

"Yup," she told him, looking at the browning sprouts and the slightly charred mushrooms, "perfect timing."

"I'd say that we're doing halfway decent," he said as he dropped the cubes into the pan, "considering we don't have the chef to guide us."

They both took a moment to silently appreciate the sound of everything sizzling. Jessie added a dash more soy sauce to the mix before responding.

"I think Hannah would say we're doing a more than reputable job," Jessie agreed, "although we haven't actually tasted anything yet."

"Did you talk to her today?" Ryan asked. "Did she say how Kat's doing?"

Ryan was referring to the fact that after the school quarter had ended last week, Hannah had insisted on staying with Kat at her place. She'd been sleeping on the couch for four nights now and spending most waking hours with her too.

Her demand to watch over Kat wasn't a total shock to Jessie, considering how close the two of them had gotten. Just last summer, Hannah had informally interned at Kat's one-woman, downtown detective agency, working with her on cases, often spending long hours stuck in a car, watching subjects do little or nothing of interest. The time together had forged a bond and Hannah, who didn't have to worry about school until the new year, wasn't about to let Kat suffer alone.

“We did talk earlier,” Jessie said. “There wasn’t much in the way of good news. She said that she had to coax Kat out of her pajamas long enough to take a shower, her first in three days.”

“How did she manage that?”

“She reminded her that she had an appointment with Dr. Lemmon this afternoon.”

Dr. Janice Lemmon was the go-to person for their family’s mental health issues. Before she’d entered private practice she was, like Jessie, a criminal profiler, who had assisted both the LAPD and FBI. Now approaching 70, the tiny woman with thick glasses and tight, little gray ringlets of hair had set aside that kind of excitement.

She had been Jessie's therapist for over a decade now, from back when she was in college. Later, she took on Hannah as a client to help her deal with what could diplomatically be called "anger management issues." She was also directing Jessie and Ryan through their couples' therapy. And now she'd taken on Kat, too, hoping to help her through the grieving process.

“Did Kat go to the appointment?” Ryan asked.

“She did,” Jessie answered, as she dumped the red onions in the pan, “but I don’t know how well it went. I know she’s still fixated on Ash Pierce, even though the woman wasn’t behind Mitch’s death. I’m hoping she’s eventually able to move past that.”

“Speaking of his death,” Ryan said, taking over mixing duties from her, “I spoke to Captain Parker about that earlier. Even though Haddonfield’s manifesto was taken down, she’s worried that Jimmy Platt won’t be the only one who tries to act on it. She fears there may be other copycats out there, and frankly so do I. I’m not sure the department has the resources to keep everyone that Haddonfield threatened safe.”

“I had an idea about that,” Jessie replied, moving over to the bottle of Syrah at the far end of the counter and holding it up to get his approval.

He nodded, before adding, “no guarantees that we’ll get to enjoy it.”

“I know,” Jessie said. “It seems like the second we pop a cork, Parker calls with a new case. But let’s risk it.”

"Okay," Ryan said. "So what's your idea?"

“I’m thinking of meeting with Haddonfield in person.”

"Wait, what?" he asked, incredulous. "You want to go to Twin Towers and chat up the guy who killed multiple people to get back at you before he tried to kill you too?"

"Hear me out," Jessie said.

Ryan sighed heavily as he moved the wooden spoon around the pan.

"I'm listening," he replied.

"I've been thinking," she said carefully, knowing he wasn't going to love this. "All of Mark Haddonfield's issues with me stem from his belief that I wronged him personally when he didn't get admitted into the profiling seminar I was teaching at UCLA."

"Which was bananas," Ryan noted.

"Agreed," Jessie said. "I had no control over that. The school did. But set aside the fact that he's an unbalanced guy who thought he had some personal connection with me, who assumed that I was going to mentor him and that he would become my profiling protégé. And press pause on the additional fact that once that didn't happen, he decided to punish me for my 'betrayal' by killing survivors that I'd rescued from previous serial killers."

"Should I also set aside that he ultimately tried to kill you too?" Ryan asked, clearly irritated by this thought experiment.

"For now, yes," Jessie replied, "because I think all of that can work for us."

"How so?"

Jessie pointed at the pan. "You've stopped stirring. It's going to burn if you're not careful.

Ryan resumed maneuvering the ingredients around the pan, and Jessie continued.

"What if I *let* him be my protégé?" she asked.

Ryan shook his head in confusion.

"I don't get it," he said. "What do you mean?"

"I mean, what if I went to the prison and met with him, told him that I'd had a change of heart and wanted his input on cases, but only if he renounced the manifesto and announced to any potential copycat that me and my loved one were off limits?"

"So in exchange for revoking what is essentially a kill order, you'd confer with him on cases?" Ryan asked, dubious.

"Technically, yes, but not in any meaningful way," Jessie assured him. "If I agreed to visit him, say once a month, and went over a case file, asked for his insights and suggestions, I'm thinking that might appeal to his neediness and his narcissism. If he knew that those visits continuing was contingent on the safety of me and my family, I think he might go for it."

"You don't think he'd suspect he was getting played," Ryan wanted to know.

"But he wouldn't be getting played," Jessie said. "I would come to him with real cases, albeit not high-profile ones, and genuinely ask for his views. That doesn't mean I have to act on anything he says. But if giving him a little personal time gets him to call off his dogs, that seems like a small price to pay."

"What about his trial for committing multiple murders and attempting to kill you?" Ryan reminded her. "It starts next month and you're a star witness. Won't that complicate matters?"

"Not necessarily," Jessie said. "I'd let him know up front that our arrangement wouldn't have any impact on the trial or my testimony. The guy likely doesn't have any illusions about whether he'll be spending the rest of his life behind bars. Maybe the thought of speaking with me periodically will make that seem less onerous."

"I know it would for me," Ryan said with a wry smile, removing the pan from the stove and turning off the heat. "But what if he gets assigned to prison far away, say Corcoran or heaven forbid, Pelican Bay? That place is all the way up near the Oregon border."

"I'd tell him that my job responsibilities would keep me from visiting as often, but that within the bounds of my work obligations and prison rules, I'd still meet with him semi-regularly."

"Is this something you're willing to do for the rest of his life?" Ryan pressed.

"We'll cross that bridge down the line," Jessie answered. "Right now, I just want to secure the safety of my loved ones. And who knows, maybe after meeting with me for a while, he'll be too emotionally invested to re-issue any calls to harm me or the people I care about."

"That might be wishful thinking," Ryan told her as he spooned dinner onto her plate.

She shrugged as she poured wine into the two glasses on the table.

"It's better than doing nothing and waiting for the next shoe to drop," she said, sitting down across from him. "Now let's dive in."

She raised her glass. Ryan did the same. They clinked briefly and took their first sip of the wine. Jessie stabbed the first bite of the steaming hot meal and was just putting it in her mouth when Ryan's cell phone rang. He held it up for her to see. The call was from Captain Parker.

"You've got to be kidding me," Jessie muttered.

Ryan smiled ruefully.

"Maybe she just wants to say 'hi.'"

CHAPTER TWO

Parker didn't just want to say "hi."

As Jessie and Ryan quickly learned, she wanted to assign them a murder case.

Jessie sighed silently as the captain gave them the address and asked them to head over to the crime scene immediately, saying she'd give them the details in the car. That meant that Jessie had two minutes to scarf down some dinner, change out of her sweats and back into something professional.

She gave herself a quick once over in the bedroom mirror to make sure she was presentable. She wore the same gray slacks from earlier that day, but with the temperature dipping into the low 40s tonight, she switched to a black wool sweater and tossed on a coat.

She pulled her shoulder-length brown hair out of her green eyes and tied it back into a ponytail. Then she slipped back into a pair of brown sneakers, which looked like loafers, and added an inch to her already considerable five foot ten height. Satisfied, she headed out the door and hopped in the car. Ryan drove while she called Parker back.

"We're en route, Captain," she said once Parker picked up the line. "What's the situation?"

Jessie had learned not to waste time on pleasantries with Gaylene Parker. The woman was the epitome of no-nonsense. A forty-four-year-old mother of two, she had worked her way up from street officer to an undercover detective with the Vice unit, where she often posed as a prostitute. Eventually, she was promoted to head up the unit, which she led for four years.

It was only when Ryan gave up his position as captain of Central Station to return to running HSS and recommended her as his replacement that she took over the job. Adapting to her leadership style had been challenging for both Jessie and Ryan. She was professional but brusque, and as captain, more fixated on adhering to department policy than Ryan had been. Both of them, but especially Ryan, had felt the friction.

"You're victim's name is Tabitha Reynolds," Parker replied without preamble. "The officer in charge on the scene, Sergeant Kenton, will give you all the details. But the short version is: she's a fashion influencer and blogger with several million followers, which alone would be enough to make her fit the HSS case criteria. But apparently, she was also murdered via some kind of aerosolized poison. They hadn't determined exactly what kind the last time I checked. That combo made it seem like a perfect fit for you two."

"All right," Ryan said. "At this hour, we should be there in about twenty-five minutes. Maybe the folks on scene will know more by the time we get there."

"Keep me posted," Parker instructed. "I haven't heard from Chief Decker yet, but the murder of a high profile person using a poison spread through the air? It's only a matter of time before I get the call. I want to be prepared with some answers."

"Got it," Ryan said before he realized he was talking to a deadline. Captain Parker had already hung up.

"Good thing she a cop and not a doctor," Jessie said. "Her bedside manner leaves a lot to be desired."

***

They made good time.

It only took twenty minutes to get to Tabitha Reynolds's Venice loft. It was just six blocks from the beach, in an arty-industrial section comprised of converted warehouses. Ryan parked down the block from her building. There wasn't much choice as the area all around it was swarmed with police cars, fire trucks, an ambulance, and even a hazmat truck.

They walked over but didn't even get close before a young officer held up his hand.

"Sorry folks, this is a crime scene," he said, managing to sound appropriately apologetic.

"Detective Ryan Hernandez," Ryan said, holding up his badge and ID. "This is Jessie Hunt. We're working this case."

"I understand, Detective," the officer said, "but I'm still not permitted to let anyone past this point without express authorization from Sergeant Kenton. Let me tell him you're here, and he can assess how to proceed."

They waited while the young officer spoke into his two-way radio.

"I know Kenton," Ryan quietly said to Jessie. "Back when you were restricted to desk duty because of your head injury and Susannah

Valentine was my partner on that case with victims dumped under freeway overpasses, he was the officer in charge on the scene. I remember him being pretty solid."

As if on cue, Jessie watched as a burly thirty-something cop with bushy, black hair headed their way.

"Good to see you again, Detective Hernandez," he said more casually than one might expect under the circumstances.

"You too, Sergeant," Ryan replied, shaking his hand. "This is Jessie Hunt, our profiler. She'll be working the case with me."

"Your reputation precedes you, Ms. Hunt," Kenton said, shaking her hand as well. "Here in Pacific division, we're all big fans of your work."

"I appreciate that," Jessie said, always uncomfortable with praise unless it advanced a case. "I gather that hazmat truck has something to do with why we're not allowed on the scene?"

"That's correct," Kenton said. "Those guys are keeping a pretty tight lid on things until they're sure the area is safe. I was wearing a gas mask until two minutes ago, as is everyone still in the loft right now, including the CSU folks and the coroner. They think it'll be at least another hour before we're all clear to enter without one."

"That makes it a little hard to evaluate the crime scene," Ryan noted.

Kenton nodded sympathetically as he pulled out his phone.

"When I heard you were assigned to this case, I figured you might feel that way," he said. "So I took multiple photos to at least get you started. I'm also happy to fill you in on what we know so far."

"Please do," Jessie replied.

Kenton held up his phone to show them pictures as he spoke.

"The victim is Tabitha Reynolds," he said, displaying a photo of a naked woman with a towel wrapped loosely around her, lying on a bathroom floor. Her body was rigid and contorted and her right hand was extended out, clutching her bathmat, about four inches from a phone just beyond her reach. Her platinum blonde hair was still wet, and her brown eyes were open. "She was thirty-seven years old, divorced with a child who was out of town with her father at the time of death. She'd been living here for about a year."

Jessie could almost physically feel the pain and panicked horror that Reynolds must have experienced in her last moments. The woman's eyes were frozen in anguish, as if her last thought had been that she'd never see her child again. Jessie looked away, trying to regain her composure. She needed to be clear-headed to get justice for Tabitha Reynolds.

"Was she trying to make a call?" Ryan asked.

"We think so, but that the poison got to her before she could."

"Tell us about that," Jessie requested, her voice quiet.

"We believe this canister was used to dispense it," Kenton told them, flipping to another photo and pointing to an unmarked, silver, metal cylinder on the counter. "Our initial examination suggests that it both has a timer and is motion-activated."

"What was the poison?" Ryan wondered.

"The coroner wasn't willing to commit definitively when I left him. He may know more now."

"Okay, what can you tell us about Reynolds?" Ryan asked. "We understand she's in the fashion industry."

"According to the friend who found her, Marnie Krebs, that's an understatement," Kenton explained. "She used to be a stay-at-home mom, but after her divorce she apparently threw herself into her passion, which was fashion. In less than two years, she's established herself as a major player in the industry. I'm hardly an expert, but supposedly her reviews of the latest lines, which can apparently be quite cutting at times, are highly anticipated and extremely influential."

"You said a friend found her?" Jessie asked. "Where is she?"

"In that ambulance," Kenton said, pointing back toward the scene. "Because she was exposed to the poison, they decided to isolate and treat her immediately."

"Is she showing any symptoms of infection?" Jessie asked.

"Not so far, but apparently they can sometimes take a while to manifest, depending on the poison used," Kenton said. "I told the coroner, Dr. Roone, that you're here, and he said he'd be out to update you soon."

Jessie recognized the name. Dr. Michael Roone had been the coroner on their most recent case as well, involving multiple wealthy women strangled to death in their own homes.

"Until we can speak with Roone, can we at least talk to this friend, Marnie?"

"Sure," Kenton said. "The EMTs are planning to take her to the hospital, but I believe they're still evaluating her. Let's head over."

They made their way past the lookie-loos and the police tape until they got to the ambulance. As they walked, Kenton filled them in.

"She was apparently coming over for a girls' night because Reynolds' daughter was with her father. I've called him, by the way. He and the girl, Samantha, were on their way to Yosemite to go camping. He says he picked her up from the loft around noon. Marnie arrived at six, but there was no answer at the door. She called Reynolds and said she could hear the phone ringing inside. She was concerned, so she checked the door, which was unlocked. She followed the sound of the ringing phone and found her in the bathroom."

They stopped at the ambulance, where Kenton introduced them to the EMTs, then cut to the chase.

"Are Detective Hernandez and Ms. Hunt able to speak to the witness?"

"Yes, but please keep it quick," said a petite, stern looking woman wearing a respirator as she pulled open the back doors of the ambulance. "We're just about ready to transport her."

Jessie glanced inside and was stunned by what she saw.

CHAPTER THREE

Marnie Krebs looked like she was about to head into outer space.

She was wearing a full-body, protective hazmat suit, complete with a respirator of her own. Because of that, it was hard to get a clear view of the woman. Based on the hints of wrinkling in her eyes, Jessie estimated that she was in her mid-thirties. Those eyes, blue but puffy and tinged with red from crying, were wide with fear.

"Hi Marnie," Jessie said, not moving any closer but using her warmest, "you can trust me" voice. "My name is Jessie. I work with the police. May I call you Marnie?"

The woman nodded weakly.

"Thanks. How are you feeling?"

"Okay, so far," Marnie said, sounding distant behind the mask. "But they tell me it's too early to know if I was affected."

"We're all hoping that's not the case," Jessie told her. "I know they're about to take you to the hospital, but I was hoping we could ask you a few questions before then. Is that okay?"

Marnie nodded a little more firmly.

"Sergeant Kenton gave us the basics of what you told him already," Jessie explained, "but I'd like to get a few more details. We understand you arrived here at six. Did you talk to Tabitha earlier in the day, maybe to reconfirm?"

"Yeah," Marnie said. "We spoke this afternoon to talk about what we wanted to order for dinner."

"Do you remember when that was?" Ryan asked.

"I think it was around four," Marnie said. "I was still at work. I remember that I still had about an hour before I could leave. I was calculating whether I could buy the wine, get home to change, and then get over here by six. But you can look at my phone to double check the time that we spoke."

"We'll do that, thanks," Jessie assured her. "So you talked to her around four and got here at about six. We heard why you opened the door and went inside. I know this is difficult, but when you entered the loft, did you notice anything unusual?"

"Like what?"

“Anything out of place?” Jessie suggested. “Anything missing?’

“I couldn’t really say,” Marnie admitted. “We’ve been friends for a half dozen years, but most of that time was in her old house. Since then, this was the second apartment she’d lived in, so it wasn’t like she’d really settled in completely.”

“What about in the bathroom?” Ryan pressed. “I know finding her must have been horrific, but were you able to pick up on anything out of the ordinary in there? Perfume she didn’t use? New flowers?”

“To be honest, Detective, I couldn’t focus on anything other than my friend lying dead on the floor,” Marcie said. “I called 911 right away. I thought maybe she’d had a heart attack or something, what with the way she was still in her towel. It looked like she’d just gotten out of the shower. It wasn’t until the coroner guy said something about the silver can in there that I got worried that something else had happened.”

Jessie and Ryan looked over at Sergeant Kenton, confused.

“Sorry, I should have mentioned this earlier,” he said, “I was so focused on your questions about the scenes that I let it slide, but Dr. Roone thinks this case may be connected to another one he worked earlier in the week. There was an unmarked, silver cylinder found there too. As soon as he saw that, he called in the hazmat team.”

"I'm sorry, but we really need to get moving," the petite EMT insisted.

“Sure,” Jessie replied, doing her best to temporarily set aside what she’d just heard, “one more question before you go, Marnie: did Tabitha have any enemies that you’re aware of?”

Marnie shrugged awkwardly inside the suit.

“I mean, she could be pretty harsh in her fashion commentary,” she acknowledged. “Not everybody was a fan. And she had a tendency to flaunt her newfound wealth, like a lot. I know there were some haters online regarding that. But she never mentioned anybody in particular who concerned her. I feel like she would have.”

“What about her ex-husband,” Ryan wanted to know, “did she get along with him?”

“Pretty well, yeah,” Marnie said. “I would call their relationship ‘amicable.’ They wanted to keep it that way for Sammy. She once told me that she didn’t have any animosity toward him. She just felt like she was stagnating with him.”

“That’s two questions,” the EMT noted and indicated that she wanted to close the doors. Ryan looked at Jessie, who nodded that she was okay with it. It took less than ten seconds from that go-ahead for the vehicle to pull out with siren blaring and lights flashing.

Once it was out of sight, she turned around to find herself face-to-face with a man wearing a gas mask. She half-jumped until she realized it was the coroner.

"Whoa," she said. "You startled me, Dr. Roone."

"Sorry about that," he said, removing the mask, "I forgot I was wearing this. I called out to you both on the way over here, but I guess you couldn't hear me with the sirens. Sergeant Kenton said you were anxious to speak to me, so I came out as soon as I could. I assume you'd like to hear what I've learned."

Very much so," she told him.

Jessie appreciated that the man didn't want to waste their time. Dr. Michael Roone, an assistant coroner with the Los Angeles County Department of Medical Examiner, was as fastidious in his manner as in his dress. Though his voice was perpetually gravelly and tired-sounding, he spoke quickly, as if he was constantly trying to end whatever conversation he was in. As usual, tonight he was wearing a suit jacket, tie, and slacks, despite the risk of the clothes getting stained or in this case, possibly covered in poison.

"We think the victim was poisoned using an aerosolized version of a toxin called botulinum," he said.

"Isn't that what's used in Botox treatments?" Ryan asked.

"Yes," Roone confirmed. "But that's usually administered via injection and in much smaller doses. When exposed to this quantity of the poison, and in aerosolized form, it can be incredibly harmful. Remember, it's a neurotoxin. And in massive quantities like this, it can cause anything from blurred vision to muscle weakness. Without treatment, it can lead to full muscle paralysis, including the muscles that cause breathing and make the heart pump. Inevitably, that results in respiratory failure."

"Dear god," Ryan muttered. "How common is this?"

"Not very," he explained. "It most commonly occurs via foodborne transmission, and sometimes through infected wounds. Those are usually accidental. Aerosolized intoxication is much rarer and is almost always intentional. In this form, it's essentially a bioweapon. The fact that the device that expelled the poison had a timer and a motion-activated sensor would seem to leave little doubt—this was a murder committed by someone who knew exactly what they were doing and the danger of the poison they were using."

They were all quiet for a moment before Jessie asked the foremost question in her mind.

“How fast-acting is this?” she wondered. “It appears that Tabitha Reynolds barely had time to get out of the shower and certainly not enough to call for help.”

"Typically, it might take hours or even days for symptoms to become life-threatening," Roone replied. "In this instance, I'm guessing that—and I can't stress this enough—the poison was massively concentrated."

“So how exactly would this work?” Jessie pressed.

Roone scrunched up his face in concentration.

“My theory is that the killer would have placed the cylinder in the bathroom and set the timer,” he explained. “When time was up, the motion sensor was activated. Then, when Reynolds walked passed the sensor on the cylinder, the poison was expelled, exposing her. But since botulinum is colorless and odorless, she probably had no idea it was happening. She was in an enclosed bathroom. Assuming she got undressed and showered, that would have left her exposed for a while. Even a few minutes might be enough to cause her muscles to shut down. By the time she realized the extent of her situation, it was too late to act.”

Jessie pictured Tabitha Reynolds, in those final desperate moments, processing that her body was failing her and trying desperately to do something about it. Her clenched fist, grabbing at her bathmat only inches from her phone, was evidence of that.

“Sergeant Kenton said this wasn’t the first time you encountered this,” Ryan noted dourly.

Roone nodded.

“That’s right,” he confirmed. “Last night, I was called to a scene for a woman named Clarissa Langley. The circumstances were very similar. She was found in her Marina del Rey home, not ten minutes from here. Same basic situation. She was lying on the floor in her bedroom. Initial indications suggested a heart attack even though this was a thirty-nine-year-old woman in good shape. It wasn’t until the discovery of a cylinder just like the one we found in Tabitha Reynolds’ bathroom that we began to suspect something more ominous.”

“Weren’t you and your people exposed to the toxin?” Jessie asked.

"We were," he answered, "and we all underwent extensive testing after the fact. Luckily, while exposure to a concentrated dose of the poison is deadly, the toxin diffuses in the air pretty quickly. We arrived on the scene several hours after Langley's estimated time of death, so our risk was greatly minimized."

"But not here," Ryan noted. "Tabitha Reynolds might have died as late as right before 6 p.m."

"That's true, which is why we're having Ms. Krebs taken to the hospital. She's at the most risk of exposure. Our people didn't arrive on the scene until about thirty-five minutes later. That obviously put us at some risk, which is why we're all wearing masks and will get tested again later. But my working theory is that unless one is exposed within the first few minutes after the release of the toxin, the risk is severely minimized. We caught a lucky break in that no one else was in the loft at the time, or we could be looking at multiple victims here."

"Well," Jessie said, "I hate to be the one to say it, but with two victims killed using the same method, it looks like we've got a serial killer on our hands."

"Agreed," Ryan said before turning to the coroner, "Dr. Roone, we'd love it if you could send us your report on Clarissa Langley's death right away."

"As soon as I get back to the office," he promised.

"And I'll call the detectives who've been handling the Langley case," Sergeant Kenton said. "I can let them know you're taking over and have them send you the police report immediately. Plus, we're pulling any available security footage from both homes. I'll let you know what we find."

"That would be very helpful," Jessie said, "Because right now we have two victims and no good leads to follow."

Ryan sighed, and Jessie knew what he was thinking before he said it.

"I have a feeling that this is going to be a very long night."

CHAPTER FOUR

Hannah Dorsey tried not to make it obvious.

It wasn't easy. After all Kat Gentry was a professional private detective who was usually pretty good at picking up on subtle behavioral changes in other people.

So as Hannah spent much of the last four days in Kat's apartment, watching her sister's best friend out of the corner of her eye without trying to let on that she was essentially babysitting an adult woman, she did her best to seem like her usual self.

But Kat wasn't at the top of her game right now and mostly seemed oblivious to being so closely observed. It was understandable. After all, it was barely two weeks ago that Kat's fiancé, Mitch Connor, was gunned down as the two of them were leaving a movie theater.

That would have been bad enough, but Hannah knew that Kat's pain was compounded by unjustified guilt. The young man who shot Mitch, a punk named Jimmy Platt. He was committing the act at the behest of Mark Haddonfield, a serial killer Jessie had captured who had sent out a manifesto calling on followers to harm those that Jessie loved. But Mitch hadn't been the target. Kat was.

When her fiancé stepped in front of her as the gun was fired, he took the bullet intended for her. Even though she hadn't said it out loud, Hannah knew that Kat felt responsible for the death of the man she loved.

In the weeks since, Kat had a circle of people caring for her as she navigated the police investigation of the crime, the funeral, and the processing of Mitch's personal effects. Jessie and Ryan were around, along with several people from the HSS team. But they all had to eventually return to work. So Hannah decided she needed to pick up the slack.

She had just wrapped up the fall quarter at UC Irvine and had planned to spend winter break at Jessie's house, where she'd spent the last two years of high school. But she just couldn't justify spending lazy afternoons lying on her old bed, scrolling through her phone, when the woman who had taken her under her wing last summer and mentored her in the minutiae of private investigations was suffering alone in her downtown apartment. So Hannah temporarily moved in.

She didn't ask for permission. She didn't warn Jessie and Ryan that she'd be doing this. Instead she had just shown up four days ago with the duffel bag she'd packed when leaving school and announced that she would be sleeping on the living room couch for a little while. Kat had offered token protest before giving in. Truthfully, she seemed relieved.

In the days that followed, they didn't do much. Yes, Kat had gone to see Dr. Lemmon twice in that time, including earlier this afternoon. But other than that, she'd hardly left the apartment, which left Hannah to do the shopping, pick up morning coffee and take-out meals, and communicate with Kat's clients, who'd all been told their cases were temporarily on hold unless they wanted to be referred to someone else.

Hannah did her best to be constantly available to Kat, which was both physically and emotionally exhausting. She hadn't realized the wear on her body until she caught a glimpse of herself in the bathroom mirror earlier today.

On the surface, she thought that she still looked presentable. With her five-foot-nine height, blonde hair, green eyes (the same shade as her sister's), and once-skinny-but- now-athletic frame, she made a good first impression. But upon closer inspection, the hair was less bouncy and vibrant than usual. The eyes had shadows under them. And she just didn't feel as strong as usual. She hadn't worked out once since she'd arrived here.

But she found the emotional component of caring for her new charge far more taxing than the physical one. She didn't realistically think that Kat was in such a bad place that she would harm herself. But she sure wasn't engaging in a lot of self-care. She had to be coaxed to shower, change clothes, and sometimes, even to eat.

Hannah was hesitant to be too forceful. After all, she was dealing with a woman who had served in Afghanistan as an Army Ranger. That was where Kat saw multiple friends killed or injured grievously. It was also where she was injured in an IED explosion that left her with damage both internal and external, including multiple facial burn marks and a long scar that ran vertically down her left cheek from just below her eye. Hannah didn't want to insult her by suggesting she couldn't handle sorrow and suffering.

Still, she'd never seen Kat like this before. The combination of grief, guilt, and dashed dreams seemed to have undone her. More troubling than Kat's depression was her growing obsession with Ash Pierce.

It was understandable. Kat had a long, unpleasant history with Pierce. The latter was a hitwoman who feigned being a client in order to lure Kat out into the desert, where she intended to livestream herself torturing and murdering her. She'd been hired for the job by a killer that Jessie had captured and who wanted payback. Luckily Hannah, who had been working for Kat at the time, arrived in time to outwit and nearly kill Pierce before ultimately, reluctantly leaving her to the authorities.

Months later, Pierce escaped while being transported from one prison to another and went hunting for Hannah. That search ended in a confrontation in a hospital boiler room, where Hannah and Kat worked together to defeat the killer. The conflict, which involved hand-to-hand combat and a knife, ended with Hannah stabbing Pierce in the neck and Kat using CPR to save the dying woman.

Pierce ended up in a coma, leaving Kat to obsess over her decision to save the assassin. She came to regret it, especially when Pierce eventually woke up claiming no memory of those recent clashes, or any of her time as a killer for hire. The last thing she said she could recall was her work as a Marines Special Operations element leader and later, a CIA asset who, according to her, conducted covert assassinations for the agency, eliminating enemies on behalf of her country.

Kat was skeptical about Pierce's amnesia, and regularly went to the secure hospital ward where she was recuperating. She befriended the nurses and tried to get proof that Pierce was lying. When, weeks later, Mitch was shot by Jimmy Platt, who was shouting "I will complete the mission begun by my predecessor. I am the assassin now!" Kat assumed he had done it at Pierce's behest and went to the hospital ward, ready to return the favor. Only Jessie talking her down last minute prevented her from shooting Pierce, which would have almost certainly led to a murder charge.

But even though Kat was eventually persuaded that Platt was acting on Mark Haddonfield's directive and not Pierce's, she couldn't let go of her fixation. In the days since Mitch's funeral, she had become increasingly convinced that Ash Pierce's memory loss was all a ruse. She believed that the hitwoman was playing a long game, either to create doubt in the minds of a future jury judging her many crimes, or to get the security contingent guarding her to let down their guard for another escape attempt.

Hannah was generally inclined to agree with her. Everything she knew about Pierce suggested she was capable of that kind of manipulation. They'd both already been the victims of the woman's skills at deception. But Kat had taken her suspicions to a different level entirely.

She'd pored over studies about the legitimacy of post-coma amnesia. She'd talked to the ward nurses, trying to learn about any behavioral discrepancy that might prove the woman was faking. She'd even tried to go back to the hospital again this week before Hannah had convinced her that it would be an extremely bad look.

She'd suggested that Kat address her obsession at her appointment with Dr. Lemmon today. So when the woman returned to the apartment, Hannah waited what she thought was an appropriate amount of time, and then broached the subject.

"Did you talk to Dr. Lemmon about Ash Pierce at your session today?" she inquired casually, as if she was asking if Kat wanted tea.

Kat shook her head.

"I wanted to, but I just couldn't bring myself to do it. I can barely talk to *you* about it. Being judged by a professional therapist is more than I can handle right now."

Hannah didn't point out that Kat, rather than being barely able to discuss the topic with her, brought it up constantly. As frustrating as it was to seemingly be the woman's sole release valve, Hannah understood. She'd been in a similar position herself.

It wasn't that long ago that that she'd discovered something unsettling about herself. Maybe it was because her and Jessie's shared birth father was a serial killer who slaughtered her adoptive parents right in front of her. Or maybe it was because she'd been kidnapped by a different murderer who tried to convince her that she should get in on the killing game too, starting with her own sister. Or perhaps it was nearly being murdered by Jessie's ex-husband, who snuck into their home and tried to take them both out, along with Ryan.

Whatever the source, Hannah had discovered an unnerving element in her own character. She had what could only be described as bloodlust. It had developed over time but fully flowered when she shot an elderly serial killer even after he'd been subdued by Jessie and Ryan. The act had given her a thrill like nothing she'd ever experienced before.

Even though the shooting was conveniently deemed self-defense, she knew the truth: she had done it on purpose, just to see what it felt like. After that, she began seeking out other confrontations in which she could mete out vengeful justice against perceived wrongdoers. On more than one occasion, it nearly led to her committing violence against people who probably didn't deserve what she had in mind.

Ultimately, she'd gone to Dr. Lemmon, confessed how she was feeling, and agreed to go to a long-term treatment facility to work on controlling her urges. It had worked on the whole, and she'd tried to channel her need to dole out punishment in more constructive ways, most recently by helping fellow college students who'd been wronged in some way.

She was modeling herself after her sister, who had admitted that she too sometimes felt the pull toward violence against transgressors but had found a release valve by redirecting those darker desires toward a more noble goal: getting justice for the victims of the offenders.

But the tickle was always there in the back of Hannah's gut, that longing to make people pay, sometime in bloody fashion. And listening to Kat go on about Ash Pierce, a woman who had tried to kill Hannah on multiple occasions, did little to temper that craving.

"I actually have a favor to ask," Kat said, snapping Hannah out of her thoughts and making her wonder how long she'd been sitting there, silently brooding.

"Okay," she replied apprehensively.

But before Kat could go on, Hannah's phone buzzed. She glanced over. It was a text from Finn Anderton, a fellow UC Irvine student and frat boy that she'd initially despised and more recently found herself enjoying flirting with. He lived down in Orange County, about an hour away.

How's everything going? the message inquired innocuously. She was tempted to respond, but with Kat sitting expectantly next to her, she instead put the phone in her pocket. The boy could wait.

"Do you want to respond to that?" Kat asked.

"Later," Hannah said with a dismissive wave. "What's the favor?"

"I know this is a big ask, but I wanted to see if you could follow up on this whole Pierce thing?"

"What do you mean?" Hannah wanted to know.

"Look," Kat said, "as deep in my own messed-up head as I've been lately, even I know that I can't be objective when it comes to evaluating if Pierce is full of crap. But you worked for me last summer. I taught you all the basics of conducting an investigation. You could review the research I've gathered and take an unbiased look at whether her condition is legit or not."

"Unbiased?" Hannah said, unable to control her surprise, "you've got to be kidding!" Don't you remember that I was in hiding at a safe house after she escaped from prison because she had a personal vendetta against me? She tried to kill me too, Kat. I wouldn't call myself unbiased."

"Okay," Kat said heavily, as if the effort of arguing was almost too much for her, "let's say that you're more clear-headed then. I haven't slept. I can't stop crying over Mitch. And I feel like every time I move, I'm covered in molasses slowing me down. You can at least offer a fresh perspective. Will you just look at what I've compiled and see what you think? I need to know, once and for all, whether this whole amnesia thing is real or not."

"I may be double majoring in Psychology and Criminology," Hannah conceded, before trying to squirm out of the request, "but I just finished the fall of my freshman year. I'm hardly qualified for this assignment."

Kat was undaunted. "I'm not asking for your help because of your academic prowess, Hannah. You know Pierce. That makes you qualified enough in my book."

Hannah exhaled deeply. She wasn't sure that she'd be any better at this than Kat. But the woman was looking at her with pleading eyes. She knew there was no way she could decline.

Besides, if taking over this project could give Kat a mental break and prevent her from going further down the rabbit hole, that alone would justify her involvement. And in the back of her head, there was another reason she considered doing it. If Kat wasn't thinking about the case, she was less likely to show up unannounced at the hospital again and do something rash.

Of course, Hannah didn't trust that depending on what she found, she might not do the same thing.

"Okay," she replied reluctantly. "I'll do it. But only because I love you."

Kat leaned over and gave her a hug. Hannah could smell the mustiness on her.

"One condition, though," she added. "You have to shower right now."

Kat smiled weakly and nodded, getting up immediately. As she watched her go, Hannah already began to wonder if she was making a terrible mistake.

CHAPTER FIVE

Jessie got out of the car and stretched.

The drive from Tabitha Reynolds's Venice loft to their current location in Mar Vista only took ten minutes. But in between they'd made a forty-five minute pitstop at a local diner to review the case file they'd been sent on the first poisoning victim, Clarissa Langley.

Jessie had noshed on a stale blueberry scone, a far cry from the chicken and Brussels sprout skillet she and Ryan had originally intended as tonight's meal. But their time in the diner had proved somewhat fruitful.

While there, they reviewed the file over the phone with the HSS researchers, Jamil Winslow and Beth Ryerson. Jamil, a short, skinny twenty-five-year-old with thick glasses and no sense of fashion style, headed up the two-person department.

He was the unit's resident genius, capable of filtering through massive databases, sorting surveillance video into manageable buckets, or making complex financial records understandable, all seemingly in the blink of an eye. His social skills didn't always match his intellectual ones, which is where his sole employee came in.

Beth Ryerson, also twenty-five, was as adept with people as Jamil was with numbers. Her perpetually chill, friendly vibe was the complete inverse of Jamil's constant, jittery intensity. And while not a human supercomputer like Jamil, she had an incredibly sharp mind, which people tended to underestimate because she was an attractive, six-foot-plus former college volleyball star.

Working together with the researchers, Jessie and Ryan quickly confirmed multiple similarities between the crime scenes. They'd also learned that the colleague of Clarissa Langley who'd discovered her body last night lived only five minutes from the diner they were in. Ryan called to see if she was home. She was, and despite the fact that it was approaching 9 p.m., invited them over, which is why Jessie and Ryan were now standing in front of her place.

The woman, Raylene Florence, lived in a six-story, cookie-cutter complex on the edge of Mar Vista and Venice. But by living on the Mar Vista side of Walgrove Avenue, her rent was several hundred dollars cheaper than if she lived on the Venice side. They buzzed her apartment at the front gate, and she let them in. They took the elevator up to the fourth floor, and Ryan knocked on her door. She must have been waiting on the other side because she opened it before he'd even pulled his hand back.

“Hi,” she said nervously, “come on in.”

She stepped aside to make way for them. As Jessie passed by her, she noted that Raylene Florence had a very diffident way about her. She was wearing gray sweatpants and a navy sweatshirt without any logo. Her brown hair was pulled back in a ponytail, and she wore glasses. She carried herself with a meekness that was reinforced by her apartment.

The entire place was a collection of inoffensive choices, from the standard issue, IKEA-style furniture to the bland floral prints on the walls. It was hard to tell yet if these was Florence’s personal style or just a woman in her mid-twenties doing the best she could within her budget.

“Thanks for seeing us so late,” Jessie said, stepping into the living room and taking a seat on a hard-backed wicker chair. Ryan took the matching chair and Florence sat on the edge of the adjoining loveseat.

“Of course,” she replied. “I was a little surprised to hear from you because I already talked to those other detectives but if it helps, I’m happy to tell you what I can.”

“As I mentioned on the phone, we’re taking over the case from them,” Ryan said. “We’ve read your statement in their report but just wanted to review a few things.”

Raylene Florence nodded and waited for their questions.

"So, just to be clear, you worked with Clarissa Langley?" he began.

“More *for* her than with her,’ Florence explained. “I’m an administrative assistant at the marketing firm she worked for, Creative Concepts West.”

“Our understanding is that Ms. Langley was a senior executive at the firm.”

“That’s right,” Florence confirmed. “She was one of the top people there.”

“So why were you going to her home?” Ryan wondered.

"She had a big presentation the next day," Florence explained. "Normally she would have just stayed at the office, but I was told that she was feeling run down so she decided to work from home that afternoon. Apparently, she called and said she'd left some materials at her desk. It wasn't pressing but she wanted someone to drop them by that evening. I was assigned to do it."

"This was last night, Wednesday," Ryan noted. "The police report said you arrived around seven, right?"

Florence nodded.

"And our understanding is that she called to request her materials around 3 p.m. that afternoon?" Ryan continued.

"I didn't get that call," Florence said. "I was just told to take over her stuff. But if that's what they said, then I'm sure it's right."

"And she was alone?" Jessie asked, even though she knew the answer.

"Yes," Florence replied. "I didn't know it at the time but apparently her husband had taken their son out of school early that day. They spent the afternoon downtown before going to an L.A. Clippers game, so she had the place to herself."

"And you discovered the body, correct?" Jessie reconfirmed.

"Yes," Florence answered. "When I got there, I rang the bell, but she didn't answer. I knocked on the front door too but still didn't get a response. I knew she was home because I recognized her car from work. It was in the driveway. I thought maybe she was in the bathroom or something, so I waited a little bit and called her on her cell. I could hear her ringtone coming from inside. I started to get worried that something was wrong. I knew it was a little weird, but I walked along the side of the house, peeking in. That's when I saw her lying on the floor. So I called 911."

"And this is how you found her?" Ryan asked, holding out his phone to show her an image taken by the crime scene folks.

It showed Clarissa Langley, thirty-nine, still in the black skirt and beige blouse she'd worn to work that day, lying on her side in her bedroom. Her sleek black hair partially obscured her face. Raylene Florence glanced at it for a second, nodded, then looked away quickly.

"What was she like?" Jessie asked, her soft tone suggesting she was more interested in getting Florence's personal impressions than something official.

"I mean, I didn't know her super well," she replied. "I know that she was considered great at her job, a real shark. No one wanted to cross her."

"Did people resent her for that?" Jessie pressed.

"I'm sure they did," Florence admitted. "I don't want to speak ill of the dead or anything, but she could be pretty harsh. She reamed me out more than a few times, not always fairly in my opinion."

"Did you ever notice anyone in particular who mentioned animosity toward her?" Ryan wanted to know.

Florence thought about it for a moment.

"There may have been people who did, but they never directly said so," she said. "Everyone I spoke with was more like me. We just tried to avoid her so as to not incur her wrath."

"So you must not have been that psyched to be selected to take her the work stuff," Jessie suggested.

Florence shrugged in embarrassment. When Jessie realized she wasn't going to get an answer to that one, she moved on.

"So did you head right over or procrastinate because of that?" she asked, wondering if Raylene Florence would pick up on the fact that she was reconfirming her alibi.

"Oh, I went right over from work," she replied adamantly. "I didn't want to delay the inevitable and have it hanging over my head. Plus, Ms. Langley knew I was the one assigned, so the later I got there, the more annoyed she'd be. I just wanted to get it over with and move on with my night."

"So when did you leave work?"

"Just after 6:30," she said. "From the office to her place took a little less than a half hour."

Though her answer was forceful, something about her manner caught Jessie's attention. She was hesitant to make eye contact and squirmed nervously.

"Raylene, I feel like there's something else you want to tell us," she said gently, "but you're hesitant to do so. If that's the case, it's better to be forthcoming now, rather than have information come out later that you can't explain."

The young woman's face turned pink.

"There is one thing," she acknowledged. "I should have brought it up as soon as I realized. But I forgot at first, and then when I remembered, I worried that I'd get in trouble."

"What is it?" Jessie asked.

"I just want to make sure that I'm not going to be charged with anything," Florence said. "Can you promise me that?"

"We can't make that kind of promise," Jessie said reluctantly. "What I *can* promise is that your motives and intent will be kept in mind. And in general, coming forward is always better for you than keeping valuable information from us. It's the withholding that usually gets people in trouble."

Florence got up from the loveseat and walked over to the kitchen counter. She picked up a business card.

"I found this slid in between the door and the frame when I arrived at Ms. Langley's house last night," she said, walking back over. "I pulled it out and was going to hand it to her. But when I started to get worried after I couldn't reach her, I just shoved it in with the work materials. I forgot all about it and only remembered when I brought the materials back to work today to return to the executive team because they needed to reassign the account. I saw the card in there and realized I should have given it to the detectives last night. I didn't want to be responsible for taking the evidence that could lead to the capture of whoever did this. I thought I might get arrested or something. But it's been eating me up ever since. So here it is."

She handed Jessie the card, who held it out for Ryan to see. It read: *Gregory Ashton, Certified Financial Advisor, You do well but I can help you do better.* That was followed by his contact information.

"I'm sorry," she said, her voice thick with shame. "I should have brought it up right away. I was just really freaked out."

"Yes, you should have handed it over immediately," Jessie agreed. "But better late than never. We'll look into this."

She stood up to indicate that the interview was over. While one could never be certain, nothing in Raylene Florence's demeanor suggested that she was being evasive about more substantial matters. Plus, she already knew about Florence's alibi before she got here. She was just testing that the young woman wouldn't vary it.

Florence escorted them out. As they walked down the hall to the elevator, Ryan took a photo of the business card and sent it to Jamil and Beth in research.

"It sounds like we might have dozens of potential suspects at Clarissa Langley's office," he noted as they waited for the elevator to arrive. "She doesn't seem to have been popular among the staff."

"Yeah, but how many of them have any connection to Tabitha Reynolds?" Jessie countered. "This was a very specific targeting of two women, using a pretty unconventional method of murder. This doesn't feel like an abused employee getting revenge. There's something more methodical and cold-blooded about it."

The doors opened and they got in. Neither of them spoke on the way down, each consumed by their own thoughts. They left the building and were halfway to the car when Ryan got a call. It was from Jamil.

"What's up?" he asked.

"The financial advisor whose card you sent me," he replied immediately. "Tabitha Reynolds is a client of his."

Jessie and Ryan exchanged shocked looks.

"Are you sure?" Ryan checked. "That was really quick."

"I'm sure," Jamil said. "I'm looking at her financials and it's not hidden in any way. She hired him last year. Apparently he specializes in wealth-building for the newly affluent."

"But he wasn't working for Clarissa Langley?" Jessie asked.

"Not yet," Jamil answered. "Maybe the card was his first step to changing that."

"Can you send us his home address?" Ryan asked.

"Doing it now," the researcher replied.

"Thanks, Jamil," Jessie said, before turning to Ryan. "It looks like we're making a house call."

CHAPTER SIX

Naomi Hackett tried to force the guilt out of her system, but it was to no avail.

No matter how hard she tried to justify it, she couldn't shake the feeling that she should be at home rather than here.

"Here" was the spartan apartment she kept in Playa Vista, only minutes from her tech company's offices. From a practical perspective, it made a lot of sense. "Home" was the palatial estate in Pacific Palisades that she shared with her husband and child. Unfortunately, commuting from the office to the house on a weekday was typically an hour-long proposition at best. And these days, that was valuable time wasted.

After all, her startup, Hackett Insights, was about to make its giant marketing push right after the start of the new year and every moment counted. Naomi was a seasoned pro, having worked in senior positions at multiple major tech companies in her career.

But this was the first time she'd branched out on her own, with her own name a selling point for the company. As part of that process, last year she'd relocated the family from Silicon Valley down south to be closer to this ocean-adjacent part of Los Angeles, known as Silicon Beach. And after recently getting a major round of funding for Hackett Insights, she couldn't afford to drop the ball when it was their resources at stake.

All of that meant that instead of being at home right now with her doting husband and adorable five-year-old daughter, she was sitting on an uncomfortable couch in the pre-furnished apartment she'd rented for the last few months, all so that she could stay close to work during the week.

She thought back to her daughter Olivia's disappointed face on FaceTime earlier tonight when she learned that Mommy wouldn't be tucking her in again and consoled herself with one fact. This would be the last night like that for a while. Tomorrow was Friday. Saturday was Christmas Eve. And then there would be a whole week where she could work from home. That was what she'd told Olivia on the phone earlier—that starting tomorrow, Mommy would be around for a whole week.

But for that to happen, Naomi really had to bear down. Even though it was approaching 9:30, she still had a couple of hours of work to do to prep for the final all-hands meeting of the year tomorrow. That's why she had called the food delivery service—to re-fuel with a late-night order of In-N-Out, which should be here in the next few minutes.

She stared at the document in front of her, trying to focus. But she must have been really tired because the words blurred together. Even though she'd just gotten up a little while ago to change into more casual attire, she decided she need to recharge again, get the blood pumping.

She tried to push herself up, using the arm of the couch. But to her surprise, her arms felt shockingly weak, way more than one would expect simply from not having eaten since 1 p.m. Her muscles were stiff and borderline unresponsive. It took all of her strength to stand upright.

Something felt off. It had snuck up on her because she'd been sitting in the same spot on the couch for the last few minutes, but now the issue was apparent. She briefly wondered if her sense of guilt over poor parenting was making her physically ill. But this was something else, something more. It felt like her whole body was shutting down.

She tried to reach down to the coffee table to grab her cell phone but felt wobbly and stopped, worried that she might topple over. Instead, she decided to focus her efforts on getting to the front door. She was friendly with Jillian, the next-door neighbor, and was sure that if she could get to her, the woman could help or at least call for some.

So she forced one foot in front of the other, feeling like the Tin Man in *The Wizard of Oz*. Suddenly her methodical steps got away from her and she found herself careening toward the door. She slammed into it much harder than expected, but to her surprise and fear, there was no pain from the collision. Her entire torso felt numb.

She attempted to reach down and unlock the deadbolt but found it nearly impossible. Not only were her fingers not working properly, but her vision was also deteriorating rapidly. She managed to press her palms together on either side of the bolt and, using their collective force, twist the deadbolt to the side.

She tried to do the same with the door handle, only to discover a new challenge. Her lungs weren't working right. She couldn't inhale normally, barely able to suck any air in through her numb lips. A rush of panic coursed through her as she realized that unless something changed fast, in a matter of seconds, she wouldn't be able to breathe at all.

She fixed all her energy on twisting the door handle with her compressed palms and managed to turn it. She clung to the handle as best she could as she lost her balance and toppled backward. The door opened as she hit the ground. In the distance, she could see the vague outline of the hallway.

But she could no longer move, or suck in breath, and just before everything turned dark for her, she had a last fleeting revelation. Her heart had stopped.

CHAPTER SEVEN

This wasn't how Jessie had envisioned her evening going.

It was approaching 10 p.m. when she and Ryan pulled up outside Gregory Ashton's house. Unlike with Raylene Florence, they didn't let him know they were coming.

Ashton lived a little inland from the two victims, whose homes were both within shouting distance of the Pacific Ocean. His small but well-manicured Culver City cottage house was in a neighborhood just off the downtown business district.

As they approached his door, with only a nearby, flickering streetlight to illuminate the darkness, they reviewed what they'd learned about the guy on their way over.

"How do we want to pursue this?" Ryan asked. "Directly challenge him on what he was doing at Clarissa Langley's place or 'engage his assistance' in trying to get to the bottom of what happened to these women?"

"We're talking about a single, forty-five-year-old financial advisor who seems to be essentially cold-calling potential clients when he's supposed to be an established wealth-builder," Jessie replied. "Even before meeting him, this guy is giving off the whiff of desperation. I'm more inclined to go at him than try to win him over."

"Have at it," Ryan said with a smile.

Jessie knew why. Her husband always seemed to get a charge out of watching her knock arrogant jerks down a peg, especially when they were potential murderers. Of course, the question was: did this guy even fit that profile?

Ryan rang the man's doorbell. After thirty seconds without a response, he tried again.

"Any chance he's making a break for it out the back door?" he wondered.

"Let's give him a few more seconds before barging in," Jessie advised. "It *is* a tad late to be calling on people."

"Who is it?" a male voice suddenly demanded from behind the door.

"LAPD," Ryan said, holding up his ID and badge in front of the peephole. "We have a few questions for you, Mr. Ashton. Can you please open the door?"

There was a brief pause before the man responded.

"How do I know this isn't some elaborate ruse to get access for a home invasion?" Ashton asked, sounding legitimately concerned.

Ryan looked at Jessie, and she could tell he was annoyed. Before he said something to exacerbate the situation, she intervened.

"Mr. Ashton, if you're concerned, you can call the department directly," she said. "Give them Detective Hernandez's badge number and ask them to verify that he's out on this call. They'll reach out to him with you still on the phone to confirm what we're saying. We can have one big conference call."

There was another brief pause, then the door opened to reveal a short, salt-and-pepper-haired man with wire-rimmed glasses. He had a beady intensity to him that Jessie suspected might help with his work but didn't make him seem like a fun hang.

"I recognize you," he said. "You're Jessie Hunt, right? The profiler?"

While she generally disliked being recognized for her past exploits, she sensed that, in this case, it might actually help advance the investigation.

"That's correct," she told him.

"I know you're legit, so I guess I can assume he is too," he said, nodding at Ryan. "What's going on?"

"Mr. Ashton, a client of yours died today," Jessie said, taking the lead. "We're following up with all her co-workers, close acquaintances, and business connections. And you're next on our list. May we ask you a few questions?"

That description was an exaggeration, as she and Ryan had so far only spoken to Raylene Florence, but Ashton didn't need to know that.

"Um, okay," he said hesitantly. "Do I have to let you in, or can we do it out here?"

"Coming in is always nice, but it's up to you," she told him. How he chose to respond could prove useful information in its own right.

"I think I'd prefer to do it out here," he said.

"All right," Jessie replied, trying to hide her suspicion. "How well did you know Tabitha Reynolds?"

He looked at her, then at Ryan. He was clearly stunned, though she couldn't tell if it was at learning about Reynolds's death or because he was surprised that they'd found him the same night.

"Is she the one who died?" he asked, his voice quavering.

"She is," Ryan told him. "How well did you know her?"

Ashton pressed his palm against the door frame for support as he answered. "I mean, like you said, she was a client. I started working with her last year when her fashion business took off. Because she'd never had her own business and she wasn't used to having so much income, she wanted to determine how best to allocate it. We set up a plan and put it into action. That's pretty much the gist of it. I meet with her twice a year to review everything and decide if we want to make any changes. I think we last met about six weeks ago, maybe early November. I can check my phone if you want."

"Please do," Ryan said.

Ashton pulled his phone out of his pocket and began tapping. As he did, Jessie looked over at her husband and partner. He was on edge, ready for anything that might happen. But based on how Ashton had reacted so far, there was no indication that he was on the verge of doing anything precipitous. Of course, Ryan had been a cop a lot longer than she'd been a profiler, so she wasn't inclined to dismiss his concerns.

"Yeah," Ashton said a moment later, we met on November 2nd. She came to my office, which is just a few blocks from here."

"Did you notice anything unusual at that meeting?" Jessie wondered. "Did she mention any concerns that you found out of the ordinary?"

"I honestly can't remember anything like that," Ashton said. "I could check my notes but if nothing springs to mind right now, then it was probably a pretty standard meeting."

"Where were you earlier today?" Ryan asked forcefully, clearly hoping to get the man out of his comfort zone.

It worked, as Ashton looked taken back.

"Um," he mumbled, unsettled. "It was a normal day, I guess. I had meetings with clients pretty much non-stop, like most days. First one at 9 a.m. Last one at 4 p.m. Then I went to an appointment with my therapist. After that I stopped at the store to get groceries for dinner and made it. I've been watching the bowl game ever since."

"Which one?" Ryan wanted to know

"The Armed Forces Bowl," he said. "Air Force versus Baylor, which is my alma mater."

"Isn't that game over?" Ryan challenged.

"It is, but because of work, I recorded it and am watching it on delay."

Jessie noted that the guy seemed to have an answer for everything.

"You seem to have a pretty packed schedule with all your client meetings," Ryan continued, undaunted. "I'm wondering where you find the time to hand-deliver business cards to potential clients."

"What?" Ashton asked, either truly confused or feigning it quite well.

"Your business card was found slid into the door of a woman in Marina del Rey," Ryan informed him. "I'm trying to understand why a successful financial advisor like yourself would go so far afield to put cards in the front doors of random people's homes."

"I didn't," Ashton insisted, sounding offended.

"Then how do you explain this?" Ryan pushed, holding out the card.

Ashton stared at the card for a moment before a sense of recognition appeared to come over his face.

"I think I know what's going on here," he said. "I periodically do a refresh of potential, new clients. I have certain markers I use to determine who might be a fit. If I don't know them, I try to use shared connections to make contact. If I don't have one of those, I'll try calling them. If that fails, I have a guy I send out to personally deliver cards to their homes. It's a little old school and admittedly not the most upscale method of securing new clients. But these are tough times and I've had success with it in the past, so I'm not above it. But I never personally go to anyone's home. If you tell me where you got this card, I can explain why I selected the person."

"The name is Clarissa Langley," Jessie said, sensing that this lead wasn't as promising as it had seemed several minutes ago.

Ashton punched it into his phone.

"Oh yes," he said. "I remember now. I heard through a client of mine who works at Creative Concepts West Marketing that she wasn't happy with her advisors. I tried to reach out to her using his name but never heard back. This was a last-ditch attempt before I crossed her off the list. Why are you asking about her? And what does this have to do with Tabitha? Did this Langley woman complain? Because I make sure my guy never violates any property or privacy laws."

"She's dead, Mr. Ashton," Ryan told him.

The man began blinking uncontrollably and fumbled with his phone. It fell from his hand. Jessie reached out and snagged it just before it hit the ground.

"Thank you," he said, taking it back from her. "I'm sorry, but this is a little overwhelming. I see why you're here now, but I can assure you, I've never met Ms. Langley. My notes say that I left her two voicemails, which she never returned. Other than that and sending my man to deliver the card, I've never had anything close to personal interaction with her."

Ryan was about to respond when his phone rang. He pulled it out and looked at the screen. Jessie saw his face sink as he stepped away to answer it. Jessie returned her attention to Ashton.

"We're going to need you to provide a detailed, verifiable accounting of your whereabouts from four to six this afternoon, as well as for Wednesday from three to seven. Send all of it to Jamil Winslow at this number," she said, handing over a card of her own.

Ryan hung up and stared at her urgently.

"We need to go," he said.

Jessie nodded before turning to Ashton. "Get all that information to Winslow in the next hour. Got it?"

Ashton nodded that he did. Without another word, she turned and headed back down the path to the car. Ryan fell into step beside her. She didn't need to ask to know what had happened. Someone else was dead.

CHAPTER EIGHT

Jessie cringed at the sound of the siren.

Ryan had turned it on so that they could make better time to Playa Vista, where the latest victim had been discovered. But after a few minutes it became clear that at this late hour, they didn't really need it. He turned it off just as they got a call from Jamil.

"I'm hoping that you're calling because you've got updates for us," Ryan said.

"That depends on how much you already know," the head researcher replied.

"All Captain Parker said was that there was another victim, this time found in an apartment in Playa Vista. Same M.O. as the others. She texted me the address. That's all we know."

"Okay," Jamil said, "we can flesh things out for you a little bit. Do you want to start, Beth?"

"Sure," Beth Ryerson, the junior researcher, replied. "So our victim's name is Naomi Hacket, age 33. She and her family moved here from the Bay Area last year, where she had worked at both Google and Facebook. The odd thing is that her primary residence is in Pacific Palisades. The apartment where she was found was on a six-month lease."

"A secret love nest?" Ryan proposed.

"I don't think so," Jamil said. "The apartment is less than a quarter mile from her new company's offices and the rental is prominently listed in the financials. It doesn't look like she was trying to hide anything from her husband. In fact, the rental listing data semes to suggest that she used the place as a crash pad during the week, which would make sense."

"Why is that?" Jessie wondered.

"Well, it looks like her company, Hackett Insights, is launching in the spring," he explained, "but they have a huge marketing push planned for right after the New Year. Hackett was a first-time CEO. This company is her baby. It's possible that she was just burning the midnight oil to get ready and figured that driving back and forth to the Palisades every weekday was too much of a hassle."

"I wonder how much her family loved that," Jessie mused. "Did she have kids?"

"Yes, one," Beth answered. "A five-year-old girl named Olivia."

"That can't have been easy," Jessie mused before muttering almost to herself. "It won't be fun giving them the death notification."

Ryan nodded in agreement before posing another question.

"What does the husband do?"

"He's an environmental lawyer," Jamil said. "His firm has offices in the Bay Area and down here, so it doesn't look like the move impacted his work too much."

They were all quiet for a moment. Jessie watched as they zipped past other cars on the 90 Freeway. Even though Ryan had turned off the siren, he'd left the cherry light in place to alert other vehicles to their presence. At this rate, they'd be at the apartment in less than a minute.

"Hey guys," she said as a new thought occurred to her. "You said that Naomi Hackett was planning a big marketing push for the company at the start of the year. Any chance that Clarissa Langley's firm was involved?"

Nobody replied at first, which told her the idea hadn't occurred to either of them.

"We'll check and get back to you," Jamil said.

"Okay," Ryan replied. "We're almost to her place, so just text us when you know."

"Nice work, you two," Jessie added. "It's good to have this background when we go in there."

They hung up just as Ryan pulled off Jefferson Boulevard. They could see the massive residential section of Playa Vista, a huge mixed-use community that sprouted up, seemingly out of nowhere, in less than two decades.

"*If* we go in there," Ryan said quietly.

"What?" Jessie asked, not getting the reference.

"You said this background info will be helpful *when* we go in there," he reminded her, "but if this crime scene is anything like the others, we might not be let in at all."

***

Ryan turned out to be right.

Not only were they not allowed inside Naomi Hackett's apartment, but the entire building had been evacuated. They found Sergeant

Kenton, who was having as busy a night as them, standing just outside the police tape. He looked like he'd been waiting for them.

"I'm sorry we have to see each other again under these circumstances," he said, speaking aloud their shared sentiments.

"Agreed," Ryan said. "What can you tell us so far, Sergeant?"

"Before we address the situation here, I wanted to update on something we learned from the prior scenes," Kenton said. "As promised, we got all the footage from the security cameras at those residences. Our initial pass came back negative for anything overtly suspicious. It's all been sent to your team at HSS for a more comprehensive review. But I looked at it myself, and there's no sign of anyone entering or even approaching either home immediately prior to or in the window of death. Of course, with everything going on, I wasn't able to look back much further than that. And we don't have anything from here yet, though I doubt we'll have much more luck."

"Thanks for checking," Jessie said. "We'll have our people go back quite a while beyond that. It's sounds like, with the timer and motion sensor components on the canisters, they could have been placed in these homes hours, or even days in advance of being activated."

"That's a lot of potential suspects," Ryan said, before returning his attention to Kenton. "What's the status here?"

"As you'd expect, the hazmat team is still clearing the apartment. Neither CSU nor the coroner has been allowed in yet. But they did find a canister like the ones at the other victims' residences. And at my request, they did take some photos, which I have here for you."

He pulled out his phone and showed them. The first image on the screen was of a woman lying on her back just inside the entryway of her apartment. She had curly, auburn hair and pale skin that was likely only partly a result of spending so much time inside an office of late. She was dressed in loose, beige linen pants, a Cal Tech t-shirt and fuzzy socks. Kenton flipped through several additional photos of the body and the apartment, but nothing jumped out at Jessie.

"Was the door open when you arrived?" she asked.

"It was, but we weren't the first ones here," he said. "Apparently, a food delivery driver named Juan Hinojosa was. He said he was bringing her an order of In-N-Out. When he walked down the hallway, he saw the door open and her lying there like that. He said he called out to her, even tried to shake her to wake her up. But he got no response. He checked her pulse but couldn't find one, so he called 911."

"Where is he now?" Ryan asked. "Can we talk to him?"

"The EMTs took him to the hospital about ten minutes ago," Kenton said. "Even though he was only in the apartment for a minute or so, they wanted to get him checked out. But I was able to speak to him briefly before they left. I recorded part of it, figuring you might want to check it out."

"Sergeant Kenton," Jessie said, impressed, "You read my mind."

Looking slightly sheepish, he swiped to the video and hit play without replying. The interview appeared to take place outside the building, not far from where the three of them now stood.

"So, what time did you get the delivery request?" Kenton asked as the video picked up mid-conversation.

The delivery driver, a skinny, Latino man wearing an L.A. Dodgers cap who looked to be barely into his twenties, looked at his phone.

"It came in at 9:02," the man recounted. "I was near the Marina del Rey In-N-Out location, so I got assigned the order. I collected it from the drive-thru at 9:19. I arrived here just after 9:30. I texted the customer to let her know I was here in case she wanted to come down and meet me at the building's main door, but I didn't get any response. I tried again a couple of minutes later. I still didn't hear back, but someone was coming out of her building, so I rushed in before the door locked. The unit number was in the delivery request, so I took the elevator up. That's when I saw her."

"So to be clear," Kenton reviewed. "You got the order request at 9:02. What time did you send the first text to let her know you were here?"

Hinojosa looked at his phone again.

"9:32."

"We need to take him in now, Sergeant," someone off-camera said.

"That's one of the EMTs," Kenton explained to Jessie and Ryan. "He was getting anxious."

On camera, the delivery driver looked back and forth between the EMT and Kenton, apparently unsure what he was supposed to do next. Kenton resolved that for him.

"Okay, I'm almost done," he said to the EMT before focusing on Hinojosa again. "You already explained off-camera what you did when you found her. Now tell me what you did after you called 911."

"I knocked on the door of the next-door neighbor," the young man explained. "I didn't want to just be standing out in the hall near an open apartment with what seemed to be a dead woman. If someone saw that, they might think I did it."

"Did the neighbor answer?"

"Yeah, it was *that* woman," he said, pointing somewhere off-camera. "I showed her the lady on the floor, said I thought she was dead, and told her I'd called 911. She kind of freaked out, ran in the lady's apartment and started doing CPR. But she stopped after a while. I think she realized it was no use."

"Okay, that's it," the off-camera EMT demanded again. A moment later, the video stopped.

"I managed to confirm the details of his story with the neighbor, whose name is Marjorie Attell. Once the EMTs found out that she'd been in the apartment and even given Naomi Hackett mouth-to-mouth, they moved fast to get her looked at, so I didn't get any video of our conversation. But she did tell me that Hackett had only been living here a few months. Apparently she runs some new tech company that's launching early next year, and she got this place so she could spend some weeknights here rather than go back to her home in Pacific Palisades."

Jessie was glad to hear that the neighbor's version of events matched Jamil's theory and was about to ask a question when she and Ryan received a simultaneous text from their head researcher. It read: *Clarissa Langley's marketing firm was working on the launch of Hackett Insights. She was the lead strategist. Efforting more details.*

Jessie looked up at Ryan, who was clearly as intrigued as she was. Still, she asked Kenton the question she'd had before the text.

"Did Marjorie Attell offer any impression of Naomi Hackett—her personality, what kind of neighbor she was?"

"Only briefly," Kenton told her. "She said that Hackett was nice, though she always seemed harried. Apparently, Hackett felt guilty because she had to spend so much time away from her family, especially her daughter. She was excited because after tonight, she would be spending the rest of the year at their house. That was all I was able to get out of her before she was whisked away."

Jessie did her best not to reveal the deep well of anguish that suddenly washed over her. It was one thing to see Naomi Hackett's dead body on the floor of her apartment. But imagining her young daughter, waiting in vain for her Mommy to return home for Christmas? It was almost too much to bear.

"Okay," Ryan said, more focused on the facts of the situation than the emotion of the moment, "so we know that Naomi Hacket was alive at 9:02 to place her delivery service order but had died by the time that

Juan Hinojosa arrived with the food at 9:32. That's a really small window of time for this poison to take effect."

Jessie set aside the pain she knew Olivia Hackett was soon in for and nodded, adding to the point.

"Maybe that's why, unlike the other two victims, she was able to at least get to her front door. It's possible that the poison hadn't fully overwhelmed her system at that point. But something must have happened in the interim to prevent her from getting outside. Maybe the effort to get to her door used up all the strength she had. Or maybe she fell and couldn't get back up to reach her neighbor's door."

"Hopefully the coroner and crime scene folks will have some answers on that by morning," Kenton said.

"Not until then?" Ryan asked, surprised.

"It sounded like it was going to take more than a few hours," the sergeant replied. "The hazmat folks wanted to take extra precautions because the aerosol canister seemed to have been activated so recently."

"So what are we supposed to do in the interim?" Jessie asked.

Ryan shrugged in shared frustration..

"I guess all we can do is make sure that research gets all this info so they can input it in the databases," he replied. "Hopefully something will pop. Other than that, I think our best bet is to get some sleep and start fresh in the morning."

Jessie fought back a snort. The idea that she could get any sleep when there was someone out there, poisoning unsuspecting women in their own homes, was ridiculous. But telling Ryan that wouldn't do any good. He'd just worry about her. So she kept it to herself and hoped that the morning would bring some good news.

CHAPTER NINE

Hank Costabile was grinding his teeth again.

He tended to forget that he was doing it until the headache kicked in, which was happening now. He knew he should get a mouthguard to help with the issue, but that was the least of his concerns at the moment. He was more focused on ending Jessie Hunt.

There was something cathartic about knowing that he didn't have to bide his time any longer. Now that he'd made the decision to follow through on his plan for payback, all the little things that had been bothering him the last month seemed too small to worry about. Then again, he was still grinding those teeth, so maybe he wasn't as relaxed as he thought he was.

He suspected that the remaining tension he felt was more about the job he had to do than the indignities he'd suffered up to this point. And there had been a lot of the latter.

It wasn't that long ago that he, formerly a decorated LAPD sergeant, had been incarcerated at the California State Prison in Lancaster, where he'd spent eighteen months of a twenty-year sentence. He'd been convicted on charges that included trying to impede an investigation into his former boss, who had been paying an underage porn actress for sex, as well as attempting to have Jessie Hunt, the profiler investigating that porn actress's murder, killed.

While the allegations may have been "officially" accurate, he still seethed at how he had paid the price for protecting that thin blue line. It was only a technicality involving inadmissible evidence at his trial that led to him being freed on the day before Thanksgiving.

Of course, "freed" was a relative term. In his case, it meant that he was being surveilled day and night by plainclothes officers assigned to the job by none other that LAPD chief Roy Decker. That wasn't a surprise to Hank.

After all, Decker was once the captain at Central Station, where HSS was based, and according to people in the know, the old man considered Jessie Hunt the daughter he never had. As a result, he was using precious department resources to protect her from any potential threat from Hank. And he was smart to do so.

Hank had been nursing his hatred for Hunt ever since his conviction. It fully flowered while he was in prison, where he had little to do other than pump iron, avoid getting shivved, and fantasize about how he would kill her. And now that he was out, that hatred had overflowed the pot, consuming almost all of his waking thoughts.

He'd had to watch her celebrity status grow while he was behind bars. The entire city viewed her as a guardian angel of sorts, the one who could keep Los Angeles safe where others failed. It was disgusting. The truth was that Jessie Hunt was a nosy, self-righteous bitch who needed to be put down. And he was just the man for the job.

He knew that there were people in the police department and city government at large who agreed with him. Some had gotten word to him through intermediaries. Others told him directly.

But up until very recently none of them were willing to do anything about it. No one would actively help him out of fear of being discovered by Decker.…until now. One of his old confidential informants, an ex-con as bald and thick-bodied as Hank, had offered his assistance. In addition, he'd learned from a former colleague in Valley Division named Trevor Tinsley, who frequented the same bar as him, that a dispatch sergeant at Central Station resented how many resources at the station were devoted to HSS priorities.

According to Tinsley, who was now Deputy Chief of Operations, that dispatch sergeant, whose name was Crowley, was able to track Hunt's whereabouts when she was working a case. He'd agreed to keep Hank updated on her movements so that he could assess when she was most vulnerable and make his move.

But even if Hank got to Hunt at the perfect moment, taking her out would be a challenge. He'd learned the hard way not to underestimate her. She was smart. She knew how to use a gun. She could fight. And even though he was aware that she'd recently had brain surgery, she still looked to be in good shape.

Of course, so was Hank. He studied himself in the bathroom mirror of his crappy studio apartment. He admired his gleaming bald head, his thick, muscled biceps and forearms. He was proud of his massive chest, which seemed to jut forward independent of the rest of his shredded body.

But he refused to get too cocky. After all, Jessie Hunt wasn't alone. She worked her cases with her husband, Captain Ryan Hernandez, who was no pushover. He was as physically formidable as Hank, despite the fact that Hernandez hadn't spent every afternoon for the last year and a half in a prison yard lifting weights.

No, Hank would need to show the proper respect to these people, even if he despised them. If he wanted to get his vengeance, he needed to stay vigilant. Only then would he get the opportunity to grab Jessie Hunt and rip her head right off her shoulders. He imagined himself bathing in the spray of blood as it shot out of her neck like an open fire hydrant. His mouth watered at the thought.

He ordered himself to calm down. The time for that would come. But until then, he needed to keep cool. He tried to focus on his escape route for after the deed was done. Hank had no intention of returning to prison and he'd prepared an elaborate strategy to get out of town and to a country where he couldn't be extradited.

The biggest obstacle to that, and to getting close to Hunt, was these damn cops that Chief Decker had assigned to keep tabs on him. When he got the word from the Central Station dispatch sergeant, he had to be ready to shake his tail.

But as with everything else, he had a plan for that too. Hank rubbed his bald head, excited for what was coming, excited to finally deliver justice long delayed.

CHAPTER TEN

Jessie got almost no sleep.

It wasn't a surprise, but it was a disappointment. With enough coffee and adrenaline, the dull cloud hovering around her brain would eventually go away for a while, but right now she was struggling.

As she sat in the passenger seat of the car at 7:38 a.m., sipping her coffee while Ryan drove them into the station, she tried to get her bearings. Her husband knew better than to chat her up right now, so they made the trip in silence. Of course, exhaustion wasn't the only reason she wasn't feeling especially chatty toward her husband.

Though she didn't say it, Jessie was feeling a little residual resentment from last night. When she came out of the bathroom and slid under the covers beside him, she found him watching some show with videos of cute babies doing silly things.

It was almost certainly innocuous, and Ryan seemed to only be half-watching as his eyes opened and closed lazily. But some small part of her couldn't help but wonder if putting on the show in the first place was his passive-aggressive way of reminding her that they hadn't addressed the prospect of having children in a while.

She knew that she wasn't being fair. He could have simply turned on the TV and been staring thoughtlessly at the screen. He never laughed at what he saw. He never made mention of it, simply turning the TV off when she joined him. But she was annoyed, nonetheless. She'd brooded over it until she finally drifted off into fitful, unsatisfying sleep.

But as she sat in the car's passenger seat this morning, recalling that moment, her annoyance gave way to guilt. After all, she had yet to tell him that recent testing revealed that despite her miscarriage and multiple injuries, she could conceive. She'd gotten that information almost two weeks ago, and yet she hadn't mentioned a word to him. That wasn't exactly a sign of being a communicative partner.

Literally shaking her head at the thought, she tried to get out of her mental rut by shifting her focus. It occurred to her that she hadn't checked in with either Hannah or Kat yet today and decided it was time to do so, before the morning got away from her. She tried Kat's number.

"Hey," her friend answered after the second ring, "checking to make sure I'm still here?"

"That's not as funny as you think it is," Jessie chided gently.

"Sorry," Kat replied. "You're sister's out getting us some coffee so my brain isn't yet able to filter out the inappropriate jokes."

Jessie sighed.

"I appreciate the gallows humor," Jessie told her, "but it's less effective when I'm not there to see the smirk on your face."

"But haven't you already checked in with our favorite babysitter to see how close to the edge I am?" Kat asked, referencing Hannah.

Now Jessie did allow herself a little laugh.

"Not yet today," she said. "But don't worry—I'll confer with your minder soon enough. Do you want to give me your version of things?"

"Not much to tell," Kat replied unconvincingly, "Just trying to get through each day, hoping the next one is better than the last. So far, it hasn't worked out great."

Jessie heard a voice in the background and knew that Hannah had returned.

"Your sister's back," Kat told her, "and I have to run to the bathroom. Should I hand off the phone to her?"

"Sure," Jessie said, deciding not to press her friend for more information she clearly wasn't ready to share right now.

"Thanks for checking in, Jessie," Kat said earnestly, before adding, "I'd ask how you're doing but I really have to pee. Talk later?"

"Sounds good."

A moment later, Hannah was on the phone.

"How's it going, big sis?" she asked.

"Getting by," Jessie answered. "Working a new case. Heading into the station to see what broke overnight."

"The poison murders?" Hannah asked knowingly.

"You heard about them?" Jessie said, slightly surprised.

"Just what I saw online and on the local news," Hannah said. "Multiple bodies found at different westside locations. A hazmat team called in. Victims' names being kept under wraps for now. Your police peeps are being very tight-lipped on this one. Care to share more than that?"

"I don't actually know a ton more than that at this point," Jessie conceded. "We only got the case yesterday evening. We'll see how today goes. How are things with you guys? Kat wasn't hugely forthcoming."

There was a slight delay before Hannah replied.

"Sorry," she said, "just needed a moment to step outside onto the balcony. Kat may be in the bathroom but that doesn't mean she can't hear me."

"You have things to share that you don't want her to hear?" Jessie asked.

"I don't need her having something else to fixate on," Hannah said. "If she hears me whispering to you, it'll just set her off."

"You know that she's aware that you're keeping me apprised of what's going on with her, right?"

"Of course," Hannah said. "But it's one thing to know it. It's another to hear quiet murmuring and know it's about you."

"Fair enough," Jessie conceded. "So what can you tell me?"

"Well, I'm going to keep it quick because it's freezing out on this balcony and I left my coffee inside. But the short version is: I'm worried, Jessie. Kat is totally obsessed with Ash Pierce."

"Still?" Jessie asked.

"She may have accepted that it was Mark Haddonfield's manifesto which led to Mitch getting shot, not some secret order from Pierce. But she's still fixated on the idea that Pierce is faking her amnesia, and she's intent on proving it. For the record, I'm not sure she's wrong."

"Me either," Jessie said. "But I think we'd both agree that it's not the best outlet for her—to be consumed with investigating the woman who tried to torture and murder her. It doesn't feel like the most healthy use of her time. Has she mentioned any of this to Dr. Lemmon?"

"She said that she didn't," Hannah told her. "Apparently she's more comfortable confiding in me than a mental health professional, which seems…not great."

"I'm sorry that burden has been put on you, Hannah," Jessie said. "Hopefully I can share it soon. I was hoping to come by tonight or maybe tomorrow, depending on how this case goes."

"I appreciate that, but I'm good for now," her sister said. "I may actually have an idea about how to help her out a bit. You stay focused on your case. But remember, when I start up with school again, this will all be on you."

"You want to tell me about your helping hand idea?" Jessie asked, trying to hide her apprehension. Sometimes when Hannah decided to help, she ended up putting herself in harm's way.

"Not just yet," Hannah said cryptically. "I'll let you know if it amounts to anything."

Jessie fought back the intense desire to push the issue. Her sister had gone her entire first semester of college without incident. Despite her checkered decision-making history, she deserved the benefit of the doubt.

"How are you doing?" Jessie finally asked. "I know this has been a lot for you."

"I'm tired," Hannah admitted, "but I feel like being here for Kat has made a difference, so it's a small price to pay. Eventually, I'll be back on campus. I can tough it out until then.

"Well, in case I haven't said it, I really appreciate you doing this."

"You have said it," Hannah reminded her, "but it's always nice to hear it."

As she said that, Jessie's phone buzzed, indicating that Jamil was calling on the other line.

"I'm sorry, sis, but I've got to go," she said.

"That's okay," Hannah replied. "So do I. Kat just came out of the bathroom and she's eyeballing me suspiciously."

"I love you, little sister," Jessie said.

"Right back at you," Hannah told her.

Jessie switched lines and put the call on speaker.

"You've got me and Ryan, Jamil," she said. "How's it going?"

"Good morning, Ms. Hunt," Jamil said, as formal as ever. "We have some updates we thought you might find useful."

"Go for it," Ryan said from the driver's seat.

"First of all, we wanted to update you on the connections between Clarissa Langley's marketing firm and Naomi Hackett's tech startup. There was definitely regular interaction between the two. It appears that they even met once at Hackett's Pacific Palisades home. But we can't find any evidence that either woman had a professional connection to Tabitha Reynolds. That trail just dries up."

"I feel like you're holding something back," Jessie said expectantly.

"He is," Beth chimed in. "While that lead may not have panned out, we did find others that could. At various points over the last six months, each woman employed the services of both the same personal trainer and the same private tutor for their children. We have receipts and online calendar appointments that show that both of those providers were in all their homes at least once."

"That's promising," Ryan said. "Who are we talking about?"

"The personal trainer in Landon Powers," Jamil said. "Thirty-eight. Specializes in in-home sessions for extremely wealthy clients. But he's also affiliated with a fancy health club in Santa Monica. We did some online sleuthing and found that he's working from there this morning. If his interactive calendar is to be believed, he's in the middle of a training session right now and has other ones booked up through ten."

"And the tutor?" Jessie asked.

"Her name is Danielle Robertson, twenty-six," Beth said. "She's working toward getting her teaching credential, but for now, she does in-home tutoring. Just like Powers, her clients are mostly uber-wealthy. From her website, it looks like she focuses on elementary-school-aged kids. Her website calendar isn't as transparent as the trainer's. It just shows blocks of time when she's available or unavailable. No locations listed of course, considering that she works with children."

"So there's no way to know where she is now?" Ryan asked.

"Not based on the calendar," Beth conceded. "But considering that most tutoring takes place in the afternoon or evening when kids are out of school, it's possible that she's at home. Her address is in Westchester. Should we send it to you, or would you rather reach out directly?"

"Maybe send it," Jessie suggested. "I'd rather not call either of these people ahead of time. I don't want to give them a heads up. I'm thinking we go visit Landon Powers right now, since we know where he is. Depending on how that goes, we can make an impromptu stop by Danielle Robertson's place. Thoughts?"

"Sounds good to me," Ryan agreed. "Personally, I'd rather chat with this trainer at the gym anyway. If he's our guy, he's probably less likely to do something foolish if he's around a lot of other people, including a client."

"Ok then, let's go pump some iron." Jessie said. When her crack got total silence in response, she felt obligated to defend herself. "I didn't get a lot of sleep last night."

She silently hoped that her sleep deprivation wouldn't impact them at their next stop. After all, they were about to visit a murder suspect. She needed to be sharp.

CHAPTER ELEVEN

Jessie didn't love this situation.

She had hoped to catch Landon Powers in between training sessions. But with all the traffic, they didn't make it to the Pier & Harbor Club in Santa Monica's fancy Aqua Commons complex until 8:30. Powers would likely be right in the middle of his session, and less amenable to chatting. Not that they had to accommodate him, but she preferred that they start off friendly and see where things went from there. Their arrival time might make that difficult.

There was no parking allowed on the street outside the Aqua Commons, a sprawling campus that included everything from an artisanal bakery to two plastic surgery practices to a dog spa. Landon Powers's health club was on the first floor, but they had to park underground to access it. As they pulled in, a valet immediately approached them, but Ryan rolled down his window and held out his badge.

"We're going to self-park today," he informed the young man. "Where's your loading zone?"

The valet pointed to an area near the elevators.

"Perfect," Ryan told him. "I'll put on my hazards when we park. Please make sure that no one tries to tow us."

He pulled in and they headed up, where the elevator opened on a giant atrium with glass ceilings. The entrance to the Pier & Harbor Club was just off to the side. Once they stepped inside, Jessie noted that the place was essentially a large "D," curling around from the entry doors, with a hallway near the front that allowed access to either side of the facility. They were greeted by a receptionist who offered them some bottled water before asking for their proof of membership. Ryan again displayed his badge.

"We're looking for Landon Powers," he said quietly. "Can you point him out to me?"

The young woman's eyes widened, but she nodded and pointed at the far end of the gym, where it began to curve around.

"He's the blond guy in the black sleeveless muscle t-shirt," she said, "working with Mrs. Fortenbras, the woman in the purple leggings."

“Thanks,” “Ryan said before turning to Jessie. “Do you want to come along or hold back, in case he gets feisty?”

Jessie thought about it.

“Normally I’d like to be there to get his initial reaction to being confronted by a cop,” she acknowledged, “but in this case, with so many free weights lying around, maybe I’ll let you make the initial contact, just to protect my noggin if he gets feisty.”

"I like the way you're thinking, Hunt," Ryan said, smiling.

Jessie was happy to oblige on these small issues. She knew he was still concerned about her being in the field mere months after her brain surgery, and if a concession like this set him more at ease, she was cool with them.

Ryan started in the direction of Landon Powers and Mrs. Fortenbras. As he approached, Jessie took particular notice of the nature of the training session. Powers was standing behind the woman, who looked to be in her mid-forties, helping to brace her as she did bicep curls using an EZ bar.

What Jessie noted with interest was just how closely Powers was standing behind her. He was literally pressed up against her, with no space between the front of his body and the back of hers. In addition, as he guided her through the curls, he leaned in so close that he seemed to be grazing her ear with his lips as he whispered advice on what Jessie assumed was proper lifting form. It was clear that Landon Powers’s training technique was on the intimate side. Jessie couldn’t help but wonder just *how* intimate.

Ryan waited until they completed their set to engage him. Jessie saw Powers visibly stiffen at the sight of the formal-acting man in the suit jacket and slacks. She couldn’t hear what Ryan said, but even before he’d had a chance to pull out his badge, Powers suddenly made run for it, pushing Mrs. Fortenbras at Ryan and sprinting toward the main entrance and Jessie.

While his reaction was unexpected, Jessie didn't let it throw her. Instead, she stepped to the side so that the trainer had a seemingly clear path to the exit. But just as he was about to pass between her and the reception desk, she extended her right leg to the side, clipping his shin with her foot.

Powers flew forward and landed hard on his stomach. Before he could scramble to his feet again, Ryan, who had caught up by now, dropped to a knee, which he dug into the man's lower back as he yanked one of Powers's arms behind him and snapped a handcuff on his wrist. A second later, the other wrist was cuffed as well.

"What the hell?" Powers bellowed, his words slightly muffled by the carpeting his mouth was pressed down against.

"That was a mistake, Landon," Ryan said, before lifting the man to his feet, "We're LAPD and we need to have a chat."

***

Before taking Powers down to Central Station, or even a closer one, Jessie and Ryan decided to conduct their initial questioning here at the club. The manager of the place reluctantly provided them with one of their business suites. Ryan slammed Powers down into a chair while Jessie locked the door behind them.

"Listen, man," Powers began, even before he'd been asked a question. "I didn't realize that you were a cop. I thought you were Gayle's husband, and I freaked out for a second. I never would have bailed like that if I knew who you were."

"Do you often have to break into a desperate escape because well-dressed men approach you?" Jessie wondered.

"No," Landon insisted. "But this guy was walking up to me, not dressed for the gym, and had a real stern look on his face while I was…working with Mrs. Fortenbras. I guess I jumped to conclusions."

"Well, here's your opportunity to make it up to us," Jessie told him. "We understand that you've recently trained Clarissa Langley, Tabitha Reynolds, and Naomi Hacket. Is that correct?"

Powers eyed her suspiciously. "I guess it depends on what you mean by recently."

"This isn't the time to be a smartass," Ryan told him.

"Sorry," the trainer said unconvincingly, "I didn't realize it was a crime to have multiple female clients."

Ryan looked at Jessie, who nodded that he should go for it. She fixed her gaze on Powers, watching him closely.

"It's not a crime," the detective said, "but murdering them is."

Powers looked at him in disbelief, like he was making a bad joke. But when Ryan's expression didn't change, the trainer's eyes got panicky.

"Wait, are you saying they're all dead?"

"Not just dead," Ryan reiterated, "murdered. Now, is there anything you want to tell us about that?"

Powers looked at him, then at Jessie, before returning his attention to Ryan.

"No!" he blurted out. "I don't know anything about that, I swear."

"It's just that we find it odd that all three women were clients of yours," Ryan pushed. "What are the chances of that?"

"I don't know, man, but I didn't kill anybody," he insisted. "When you mentioned them all, I thought you were going to say I violated some kind of professional trainers' code or something."

"Why would we say that?" Jessie asked. "What did you do?"

"Nothing," Powers pleaded, "I mean nothing illegal. Sure, I admit that Clarissa and I would hook up from time to time. She was an attractive lady, and she didn't seem all that focused on her vows. She called me her personal stress reliever. But I mean, we were consenting adults."

"What about the other women?" Jessie demanded.

Powers paused for a second, then seemed to decide there was no point in hiding his activities.

"Tabitha and I dated on and off for a few weeks, maybe a month," he admitted. "I guess she had recently gotten divorced and was sowing her oats, you know. But it didn't work out, and it would have been awkward to keep training her, so we decided to part ways. It wasn't that big a deal, at least I didn't think so."

"And Naomi Hackett?" Jessie asked.

"That's why I thought I might be in trouble," Powers explained.

"Why?" Ryan pressed.

"We never hooked up," he answered. "I mean, there were lots of opportunities. I trained her at both her Palisades house and her apartment in Playa Vista. And I thought she might be into me, so I made a move. Turned out I was way off. She said she was happily married and that she didn't feel comfortable working with me anymore, so she ended our sessions. I thought maybe she was accusing me of something more than hitting on her, which is all it was, I promise."

"It seems like a lot of your professional relationships end up getting personal, and then ending badly, "Jessie observed. "You ever get frustrated by that? Maybe a little angry?"

"No way," he said. "Usually someone just ghosts the other person. I've never been mad about it, and no one has ever come after me. Stuff just fizzles out, you know?"

As Jessie studied the man, she had to admit that she found it hard to buy him as a killer. He didn't strike her as the kind of guy who could properly set up an aerosolized poison canister without accidentally gassing himself. Then again, she had met more than one murderer who threw off suspicion by playing dumb. Regardless of her doubts, she pressed on.

"Where were you yesterday between the hours of 4 p.m. and 9:30?"

"Um, I know that part of that time I was training a couple of people at their homes. I had a session here in Santa Monica at six and another one in Venice after that. I can give you their names if you want."

Jessie noted that those windows of time didn't exonerate him. Tabitha Reynolds had died between four and six. Naomi Hacket had passed away between nine and nine-thirty. Beyond that, the canisters' timers could have been set well in advance in order to provide him with an out. Traditional alibis wouldn't be of much help in this case.

"What about on Wednesday between three and seven?" Ryan asked, though it was clear from his tone that he was also aware of the limitations of this line of questioning.

Powers eyes lit up. "I was at a convention in Anaheim all day on Wednesday. I left at about six in the morning and didn't get back until around ten at night. Does that get me off?" he asked hopefully.

"Actually, no," Jessie said, though with each passing moment, one thing became increasingly clear. With or without an alibi, they didn't have enough to arrest Landon Powers right now.

They had to let him go. The question was: were they releasing an innocent man? Or a killer?

CHAPTER TWELVE

Avery Sinclair was easy to watch without being noticed.

For the person doing the watching, it was hard not to sneer at how the woman went about her day with unmatched arrogance, walking along in her high heels and business skirt, with her long, red hair bouncing perfectly with each step.

Slumping down behind the steering wheel to avoid being spotted in their car parked on the street, the observer took note of how Sinclair moved through the world as if it was hers for the taking, oblivious to the possibility that she might be in any danger.

As she walked back to her Porsche 718 Cayman after exiting the mansion that she was preparing to put on the market, she looked absently at her phone. She had no clue that the person who was going to snuff out her existence was less than a hundred feet away, surveying her every move.

For Sinclair, this was just another perfect mid-morning on another untroubled day, one where she could demean others, engage in petty cruelties, and still enjoy living in the lap of luxury. But what she didn't know was that these happy, easy times were about to come to an end. Someone was going to make her last moments on this earth a living nightmare. And if things went according to plan, that nightmare would end suddenly and painfully.

Avery Sinclair got in her Porsche and sped off. Her observer, parked just across the street, let her go. There would be time to catch up later.

CHAPTER THIRTEEN

Hannah knew this was a bad idea.

But even as she stepped out of the Cedars-Sinai Medical Center elevator to the fifth floor, she also knew that she wasn't going to turn back. She'd promised Kat that she would help her, and that was exactly what she intended to do.

Of course yesterday evening, when she'd started reviewing all the research material that Kat had collected on Ash Pierce, she hadn't anticipated that it would end up with her being on the same hospital floor where Pierce was being held. But as the hours wore on, she couldn't tear herself away.

Kat had compiled a detailed record of the claims Ash Pierce had made over the last month regarding her memory loss. In addition, she pulled dozens of medical research articles on amnesia, with a focus on patients whose memory loss occurred after experiencing a coma, as Pierce asserted hers had.

While the studies had a wide variance in conclusions, few of them found examples of what Pierce was claiming: that she had lost her memory of the entire time from just prior to the coma all the way back to her life as a Marines Special Operations element leader, and then as a CIA assassin, covertly targeting foreign adversaries. Conveniently, her recall excluded her later work as a hired hitwoman, which included the assignment to torture and kill both Hannah and Kat.

In the end, while Hannah was extremely dubious about Pierce's credibility, she didn't feel confident enough to dismiss her claims outright. She decided that an in-person visit was required. Of course, she hadn't mentioned that in her chat with her sister this morning. Jessie would not have approved.

Though Hannah wasn't entirely sure what her plan was, she knew her ultimate goal. She would get in to see Pierce so that she could look her in the eye, speak with her, and make some determination about whether this whole thing was real or fake.

But now, as she walked down the hospital corridor toward the secure unit where Pierce was being held, she found herself surprised.

She was feeling something that was so rare as to be alien to her: nerves, along with a bit of fear.

The last two times she'd been face-to-face with the hitwoman hadn't gone swimmingly. Last summer, she'd raced to the desert just in time to save Kat, who had been duped and tortured by Pierce. The assassin had underestimated Hannah, and she'd managed to knock her adversary out with a police baton. It took everything in her power not to keep slamming the woman's head with it until it became a pulpy mess.

Their most recent interaction, in the basement boiler room of this hospital, came after Hannah had to hide in a safe house after Pierce escaped from custody. Ultimately, Hannah got the upper hand in that encounter too, stabbing the killer in the neck with her own knife, which directly led to Pierce's coma.

The combination of experiences had led to what Hannah imagined a soldier's PTSD might be like, as just the thought of being in such proximity to Pierce was making her sweat and her heart palpitate wildly. But as she approached the checkpoint to the secure unit, where a guard was watching her closely, she took note of something else mixed in with her nerves and fear. At first she thought it was pure anger over what she'd been put through, but then she identified another emotion: anticipation.

She was looking forward to confronting the woman who had upended her life, and almost ended it. She wanted to face her down. She wanted to provide some payback. As she walked, she felt that old, familiar bloodlust licking at her heels.

"Can I help you?" the guard asked when she arrived at the checkpoint, which included a metal detector.

"Yes," she said, adopting the persona of a teenager, which she technically was, who was nervous to even be here. "I'm meeting nurse Jenny Callahan. She told me to be here at ten."

"What's the purpose of your visit?" the paunchy, thirty-something guard wanted to know, his mustache twitching slightly.

Hannah noticed that he'd done a rushed job of shaving, missing several small patches. His eyes were bloodshot, and he was perspiring slightly in his uniform. She suspected that he'd had a late, boozy night and was now suffering the consequences. She decided to use that to her advantage.

"Yeah," she said, switching into her most annoying, Instagirl mode, her words tumbling out her mouth fast and furious "so Jenny's a friend of my older sister's and when she heard that I was interested in nursing school, she said I should come by and she'd show me what it was like to be at the nurses' station. But I've been in school all this time and I'm only just now finally on winter break and I can't come in after Christmas, so this was the only day that would work. But she said she was working in the secure unit so there wouldn't be much I could see on the ward, but I said 'anything is better than nothing, girl.' So she said come on down, which is why I'm h—."

"Enough," the guard said irritably, waving his arm to shut her up. "Just put your personal items in the bin and walk through the metal detector."

She did as he asked, moving quickly so he wouldn't change his mind. Once she was through and collected her items, she added one last nugget for his benefit.

"Do you want to be in the TikTok I'm doing for my class at school?" she asked. "I could totally interview you."

"No videos are permitted in this unit," he said, sounding exhausted to still be speaking with her.

"Got it," she said perkily, noting that despite his obvious distaste for her, he was eyeing her lasciviously as she shoved her phone in her back pocket. She'd use that later if needed.

But for now, she hurried down the hall toward the nurses' station, where she encountered the woman she assumed was Jenny. In truth, she had never actually met the nurse and only knew her from Kat's description. But as soon as she saw the blonde twenty-something with the hot pink sneakers, she knew she was in the right place.

"Jenny?" she asked cautiously as she reached the counter.

"You must be Hannah," the woman said with a warm smile. "Nice to meet you."

"You too," Hannah replied, "although if that guard out front asks, you're friends with my sister and I asked to visit because of a college project."

"He won't ask," Jenny assured her. "Ernie only does enough work to stay employed. By asking you anything at all, he's already exceeded his typical security efforts for the day. That won't be the case with the folks who actually watch Pierce though."

"Right," Hannah said, glad that Jenny seemed intent on getting down to business. "So what exactly am I dealing with here?"

"Before I answer that," Jenny said, looking hesitant for the first time, "what exactly are you trying to accomplish here? Kat used to come to observe Pierce before that became a no-no. The only reason I agreed to let you come is because I felt so bad about what happened with her fiancé. I just couldn't tell her 'no,' point blank. But this is my job, and even with Kat blessing you, I can't just let you walk in there if you're planning something dramatic. I could get fired."

Hannah had been hoping to just wing this whole thing, but now that she was being asked a direct question by someone's whose employment was at stake, she felt an obligation to give an honest answer.

"Truthfully, I'm not a hundred percent sure," she admitted. "I've looked over all the studies that Kat compiled on amnesia, and I was hoping that if I could get up close and personal with Pierce, I might be able to tell if she's legit or full of crap."

"Good luck with that," Jenny said cynically. "I've been caring for her for weeks now and I still can't tell."

"You don't have a gut feeling?" Hannah asked.

"Sure I do," Jenny replied. "I think she's totally full of it, that she's working everyone to create doubt because she knows what's facing her. The longer she can make people question if she's still the same person who murdered all those people, the better chance she has of finding a way out. That's what I suspect, but have I seen anything that would definitely prove that? No, not a thing."

"Well, I may have one advantage over you in that department."

"What's that?" Jenny asked.

"This woman tried to kill me—twice. I've looked in her eyes when she tried to do it. I know the real her. And if anyone is going to make her let down her guard, even for a moment, it's me."

She neglected to include the little detail that in both those encounters, Hannah had ended up almost killing Pierce.

"Jesus," Jenny muttered. "I didn't realize that you were *that* Hannah, as in Hannah Dorsey. I just thought you were someone who worked with Kat at her detective agency. I'm starting to have second thoughts about letting you go in. It's almost malpractice for me to let you get in close proximity to someone you have this kind of history with."

Hannah shook her head vigorously.

"But that's the whole point, Jenny," she insisted. "If we're going to shake her out of her comfort zone, it's by making her face someone she has history with. It's the only way to know if she's credible."

"I don't think she'd even talk to you," Jenny said skeptically.

“Why not?” Hannah asked, coming to a startling epiphany as she posed the question. “If she’s really forgotten everything, then she’d have no reason to say no to talking with me. I’m just some girl. And if this *is* all a ruse, she’d betray that by refusing to see me. After all, it’d look awfully suspicious to refuse to talk to some teenage girl you have no personal history with. Either way, her response will be revealing. That alone is enough of a reason to try.”

Jenny’s skepticism had clearly subsided. In fact, she now looked as committed to the mission as Hannah was.

"In that case, however, this goes, you're going to need more than just your personal recollection of the encounter. Telling people that she coughed or blinked or something when she saw you won't be convincing, considering that you're not exactly objective."

“What do you propose, Jenny?” Hannah asked, intrigued.

The nurse glanced around, making sure no one else was in hearing distance.

"There's a video surveillance system," Jenny whispered. "The security team uses it for observation when there's no one else in the room with Pierce, as a safety precaution to make sure she's not secretly trying to escape her restraints. The system is normally just in "monitor" mode, but it does have a "record" function, which isn't typically used. But when you head that way, I could activate it. However, she responds, you'll have a record of it."

Nurse Jenny,” Hannah said, unable to hide her excitement, “you are an unexpected delight. Let’s absolutely do that.”

“Okay,” the nurse said, her tone more grave. “Just make sure you don’t waste the opportunity. I doubt you’ll get another chance at this.”

“Don’t worry, I won’t,” Hannah promised.

“She is in room 522,” Jenny told her. “The officer in charge is named Gaston. Tell him the same story you told Ernie. That’ll get you close. The rest is up to you.”

Hannah nodded, then turned in the direction of the room. As she rounded a corner and saw the contingent of officers outside Pierce’s door, her heart started pounding again. This was it—potentially her one and only opportunity to find out if Ash Pierce was on the level. She couldn’t blow it.

CHAPTER FOURTEEN

"Stop!" barked the thick-trunked officer with the name Gaston pinned to his uniform. "This is a secure area."

Hannah instructed her body to quake in something approximating fright. It wasn't all that hard. When she replied, she reminded herself to keep her voice high-pitched and quavery, like the uncertain teenager she wanted him to see.

"I know," she said hesitantly, though she kept advancing, "but I'm doing a school project, and I was told it was that it was okay to be here."

"Who told you that?" Officer Gaston demanded, "and stop moving forward."

"Um, Nurse Jenny at the station," she explained. "She's a friend of the family. I want to be a nurse and she said I could come check out the hospital."

"And she gave you permission to walk in this area, unaccompanied?" he asked skeptically.

"Well no," Hannah replied, not wanting to put the woman's job in any more jeopardy than it already was. "She got busy working and I just thought I'd check stuff out on my own. Is that cool?"

"No, it is *not* cool," he retorted. "Officer Braden, search her."

Another officer approached her, his right hand uncomfortably close to his gun holster.

"Ma'am, I need you to extend your hands out to the side," Officer Braden said. "I'm going to search you."

"Why do you need to search me in a hospital?" she protested even as she raised her arms, doing her best to seem oblivious to the nature of the situation.

"As I said before, young lady, this is a secure unit," Gaston retorted in disbelief. "Didn't Jenny explain what that meant?"

Officer Braden began to pat her down as she maintained a vibe of cluelessness.

"She said something about it," Hannah conceded, "but I wasn't paying super-close attention. I guess I just thought it meant that you take extra care of your patients up here, like maybe they were famous celebrities or something. But are you saying that you keep, like, criminals here?"

"She's clean," Officer Braden said, stepping away. "You can put your hands down, ma'am."

"Thanks," she said, before returning her attention to Gaston, "*Are* there criminals on this floor?"

"I'm not at liberty to comment on patients," Gaston informed her humorlessly. "You need to turn around and go back to the nurses' station. Frankly, I'm tempted to have you escorted off the floor, maybe even out of the hospital entirely."

"What's the big deal?" Hannah teased, hoping she was properly affecting 'brat' mode, "Is there someone in here so scary that I can't even know who he is. I mean, come on, are you protecting me from him or him from me? Am *I* that scary that I can't even see who's there?"

"It's okay, Officer Gaston," a voice called out. "You can let the girl in."

Hannah immediately recognized it as Ash Pierce, though her voice sounded slightly different than she remembered. It was somehow less biting, softer than before. She wondered if that was due to the knife to the neck she'd given her or some actual change in the woman's personality.

Even with the variation in vocal tone, the woman's words sent a shiver of anxiety through her, followed by surge of excitement at the realization that she was actually going to be in the same room with Pierce. She did her best to hide both reactions. After all, she wasn't supposed to know who was in there.

As she waited for Officer Gaston's response, another thought popped into her head. She wondered why Pierce was letting her in. The woman had clearly heard their conversation in the hall. If she was faking the memory loss, was she offended that Hannah asked if she was scared of her? Or if the amnesia was real, was she just curious about all the ruckus in the hall?

"It's a woman?" she managed to blurt out, remembering that she wasn't supposed to know who was in there at all.

Officer Gaston ignored her comment as he poked his head in the room. "Are you sure you want to let her in? She's a lot."

"Truthfully, I *was* going to take a nap," Pierce said, "but it'd be nice to talk to someone who's not a cop, a nurse, or a psychiatrist for a change."

Hannah watched as Officer Gaston turned the idea over in his head. She was stunned that he was even considering it. Ash Pierce was a dangerous killer, whether she remembered it or not, and to let any civilian into her hospital room would be a dereliction of duty.

But it was a disturbing testament to Pierce's personal power of persuasion that he looked on the verge of saying yes. Hannah suspected that the woman had been diligently using her time since waking up to create a rapport with those tasked with watching her and wondered if it was sincere or just a manipulation. Either way, the fact that she'd convinced the lead officer in charge of guarding her that such an interaction might be safe was beyond troubling.

"Let's keep it brief," he said tersely before glaring at Hannah. "You can stand just inside the doorway, not one step closer. Do you understand?"

Hannah nodded pliantly.

"What's your name, by the way?" he asked as he stepped to the side.

"Hannah," she replied, moving forward, hoping he wouldn't ask for the last name. She peered into the room and even before she saw Pierce, took note of the fact that there was a third, female officer seated in a chair in the corner. She eyeballed Hannah suspiciously. Hannah waved as dorkily as she could before turning her attention to Pierce.

The woman was sitting at a forty-five degree angle in her hospital bed wearing a loose-fitting, floral hospital gown. In most ways, she was much as Hannah remembered her, though there were some changes. Her black hair had been cut short. Her skin seemed even paler than before.

She'd always been a diminutive, narrow-framed woman, but she appeared even more slight than Hannah remembered. She wondered if that was because Pierce had been fed through a tube for so long. Her left arm was cuffed to the sidebar of the hospital bed, and her right ankle had a monitor on it. There was a small bandage on her neck. Hannah knew she'd had surgery to fix the damage done by the stabbing. The doctors had held off until recently because they didn't want to do the procedure while she was in a coma.

She turned to face Hannah more directly and smiled warmly at her. Her sharp, brown eyes were bright and animated. There was no overt sign that she recognized the young woman in front of her as the person she'd tried to kill twice and who had given her the injury that landed her in here. Hannah made sure to keep her own face expressionless.

"You said your name was Hannah?" Pierce asked innocuously.

“That’s right.”

“And you’re here because you want to be a nurse like Jenny?” Pierce confirmed. “She’s a friend of your family?”

“Yes,” Hannah answered, suddenly realizing the danger the nurse would be in if Pierce was faking all this and suspected that Jenny was a part of the plan to get in. “That’s what I told Officer Gaston.”

She hoped that no one would follow up on that, but if they did, her phrasing would allow Jenny to say later that Hannah had lied about their connection and that she didn’t know who she really was. Realizing that she likely didn’t have much time before this all fell apart, she decided to cut to the chase.

“Why are you handcuffed?” she asked as naively as she could.

“Because they say I’m dangerous, Hannah,” Pierce replied, betraying no hint that she accepted that proposition.

“Are you?” Hannah pressed.

"I think I used to be," Pierce replied. "They say that I was a contract killer. But I was stabbed in the neck when I was supposedly trying to kill some young woman and I ended up in a coma. When I finally woke up, I had no recollection of that or anything from the last few years.

Hannah thought she might have seen the slightest twitch on Pierce’s face when she said, “stabbed in the neck,” but she couldn’t be sure.

“I thought that kind of thing only happened in the movies,” Hannah said, with just a hint of skepticism in her voice.

“Me too,” Pierce said with a chuckle. “But now it’s my life. I’m charged with multiple murders, all of people I have no recollection of. I’m supposed to go on trial this year. It’s actually pretty terrifying, and in my view, unfair. Whoever that person was, I’m not her anymore.”

“But if you killed a bunch of people,” Hannah posited, “shouldn’t you pay for what you did, even if you don’t remember it?”

“That’s certainly what some people say,” Pierce conceded without argument.

Behind her, Hannah sensed Officer Gaston shift nervously and knew he was getting anxious. She didn’t have much time.

“Another thing, if it’s not too rude to ask,” Hannah said.

“Go ahead,” Pierce told her. “I’ve had all kinds of stuff said to me in the last month.”

“Well, I’m just wondering, how did you become a contract killer in the first place?” she asked. “I mean, you probably weren’t some bookkeeper or retail clerk or housewife before all this, right? You must have done something that prepared you for murdering innocent people?"

She allowed her tone to become slightly confrontational at the very end of that comment, hoping to get a rise out of the woman. But instead of speaking, Pierce put her hand to her mouth and coughed. There was no way to know whether it was legitimate or if she was covering her displeasure with Hannah's relentless probing.

"Sorry," she said after a moment, "still not fully recovered yet. But to answer your question, I used to work for the military in an elite unit that targeted leaders of enemy combatant forces. I remember that time vividly. I guess it trained me for what they say I did later on. It would technically make sense, even if that doesn't sound like a road I would have gone down. I remember myself as a patriot who was defending the interests of her country. I can't imagine how that would have curdled into something so dark."

Hannah had to concede that she was good. Ash Pierce was saying all the right things, whether she meant them or not. She hadn't shown any clear sign that Hannah's questioning had angered her. She projected genuine confusion at how she was in this circumstance. Nothing she'd said or done, save for that brief twitch and a conveniently well-timed cough, had suggested any awareness of who she used to be.

"Have you tried to reach out to the people you hurt to make amends?" Hannah asked, hoping that changing tactics might unsettle Pierce.

"No," she admitted. "In all honesty, I'm worried about how they might react if I tried to do that. Do you really think they'd accept an apology? Do you think they'd believe me?"

Hannah stared at her, unable to keep the coldness out of her voice when she replied. "I doubt it."

"That's what I'm afraid of," Pierce said with a guilt-ridden smile. "I think it might just make it worse."

She suddenly yawned, bringing her hand up to cover it.

"I'm sorry," she said. "I think I'm starting to hit that mid-morning wall."

"We'll have to leave things there," Office Gaston said. "Ms. Pierce has been more than generous with her time."

The way he said it made it sound like the woman was a head of state deserving of respect and Hannah was a pesky reporter he was shooing out of the room. If Pierce was suckering him, and the rest of the security detail was as susceptible to her machinations, they weren't just not up for the job, they were in danger. But she couldn't say any of that without blowing her cover as an aspiring nurse.

"Well, thanks for making the time for me," Hannah said, slipping back into the naïve student persona. "Maybe we can do it again sometime."

Pierce chuckled lightly at that.

"I doubt Officer Gaston or his friends will allow that to happen," she said, sounding regretful. "But I'm a big believer in fate. If it's meant to be, I'm sure we'll see each other again."

Hannah smiled to hide the renewed shiver that ran up her spine. Maybe the comment was intended to be harmless, a polite way for a changed woman to part ways.

But to Hannah, it sounded more like a threat.

CHAPTER FIFTEEN

Jessie didn't love how things were going.

She would have liked to have gone straight to the apartment of their next suspect, private tutor Danielle Robertson, immediately after they questioned personal trainer Landon Powers, but Captain Parker had made that impossible.

She insisted they delay that interview to give her an update on how things had progressed so far. It wasn't an unreasonable demand, as they hadn't fully briefed her since last night. The problem was that they didn't have much new to offer.

They couldn't say whether Landon Powers could be excluded as a suspect for the same reason they were having trouble eliminating anyone: the timers and motion sensors on the poison canisters meant that they could have been placed in these women's homes hours, days, or potentially even weeks before they went off.

Parker also seemed hung up on the fact that Clarissa Langley's marketing firm had worked for Naomi Hackett's tech company. Even after Ryan patiently explained that Jamil and Beth couldn't find anything to link Tabitha Reynolds to the other women professionally, the captain remained fixated on the possibility.

"Listen," Parker told them, wrapping up, "Despite all our efforts to put a lid on the nature of these murders to avoid creating a citywide panic, word is starting to get out. No media outlet has reported on the connection between Langley and Hackett so far because we haven't released the victims' names yet. No one wants to be the first to go public with that and face potential blowback. But once that's out, those companies are going to be swarmed with press and amateur sleuths trying to uncover a connection. Unless you find another theory that's more compelling in the interim, things are going to get messy."

"That's what we're hoping to do right now," Ryan told her, not fully masking his irritation. "We have a private tutor with connections to all three victims. Maybe she'll be the break we were looking for."

"Keep me apprised," Parker instructed. "In the meantime, I'll brief Chief Decker on where we're at."

As was her custom, she hung up before either of them could respond. Jessie didn't think Parker meant it to be rude. She was probably just busy. But the abruptness always rubbed her the wrong way, and she knew Ryan felt even more strongly.

"So she made us sit around for a half hour discussing leads and evidence when we could have been out there pursuing them," he grumbled as they arrived on Danielle Robertson's street. "We could have already questioned this tutor by now and maybe even arrested her."

I know Parker can be challenging," Jessie acknowledged before making an attempt at diplomacy, "but don't forget the pressure you felt all the time when you were captain of Central Station. Sometimes it makes investigations secondary to public perception."

Ryan didn't reply. She wasn't sure if that meant he agreed or was too annoyed to get into it any deeper. It was moot anyway, as they pulled up to the curb in front of Robertson's building right at 10:30.

Even though the community of Westchester was adjacent to Playa del Rey to the west, Playa Vista just to the north, and abutted Loyola Marymount University, it didn't have quite the cache of those communities. It felt older and more suburban.

The apartment complex, like many in the neighborhood, looked like something out of another era. It was in the Dingbat style, popular in in the 1950s and 60s, with retro, cursive lettering and an overhang to shield the cars parked at the front of the complex from the elements. There appeared to be about a dozen units over two floors. Despite all that, Jessie doubted that it was cheap.

They approached the locked main door to the complex. Ryan was just pulling out a credit card to jimmy the lock when a young man dashed out, apparently late for something. He was holding a suit jacket on a hangar, and his shirttails were out of his slacks. He never even looked at them. Ryan shoved the card back in his wallet as he held the door open for Jessie.

"Let's hope the rest of this is that easy," he said.

They walked around the sad little pool in the central courtyard toward the back of the building where they found Danielle Robertson's unit, #105. There was no doorbell to ring, so Ryan knocked.

"Watch," he mumbled, "we come all the way over here and she's probably off tutoring some preschooler in finger painting."

"Hey buddy," Jessie teased disapprovingly, "do you think you can set aside the grumbling for the next little bit? This woman is a potential suspect. And even if she doesn't pan out, she might have useful information about these women that could lead us in the right direction. But if she feels like you're looking your nose down at her, she might just clam up."

He was about to reply when someone called out from the other side of the door.

"Who is it?" the female-sounding voice asked.

Ryan held out his badge so it was visible in the peephole.

"LAPD," he answered. "We have a few questions for you about some of your tutoring clients."

"Hold on," the woman said before opening a series of locks including what sounded like a chain lock and a deadbolt. "What's this about?"

Jessie studied the young woman in front of them. From Jamil and Beth's research, they already knew that Danielle Robertson was twenty-six and that she had graduated from Cal Poly San Luis Obispo with a degree in Child Development.

Robertson stood about five foot five and weighed about 125 pounds, with wet, curly, sandy blonde hair and glasses that made her startled blue eyes look unusually big. She was barefoot and dressed in faded jeans and a gray sweatshirt with her college's logo on the front. She wasn't a physically imposing presence, but for the crime they were investigating, that wasn't important. She offered them a nervous, thin-lipped smile as she held the door open for them.

"I'm sorry," she said. "I only just got out of the shower a few minutes ago, and I've never had the police knock on my door before, so I'm a little thrown. I'm not sure what I'm supposed to do here. Should I invite you in?"

"We certainly wouldn't reject an invitation," Ryan said, making sure that his words didn't come across as a demand.

"Then please," she said, waving them in. "What can I do for you?"

Jessie stepped inside and looked around the living room. The place had a definite post-grad feel, with framed Ansel Adams photos and prints of famous paintings. It was as if Robertson hadn't yet determined what her personal adult style was and was clinging to the one from college until she figured it out.

It reminded her of the apartment they'd visited yesterday, belonging to Raylene Florence, the young woman who worked for Clarissa Langley. Jessie wondered if all L.A. women in their mid-twenties decorated their places the same way now. Did they have meetings about it? She decided that was a topic she could broach another time.

"We understand that you're a private tutor, is that correct?" she asked even though she knew it was. She stopped by the breakfast bar connected to the small kitchen and turned around to face the woman.

"Yes," Robertson said. "I'm planning to get my teaching credential and eventually my master's in education, but for now I was hoping to build up a little nest egg to pay for that, plus pay off some student debt."

"We saw a list of some of your clients," Jessie told her. "How did you manage to get in with such wealthy families?"

"Oh," Robertson said, running her fingers through her hair. "I was working at an upscale tutoring center in Venice and one of the moms there said she'd hire me on the side to work with her son at her home. I took her up on it, and she was happy with me, so she told some of her friends. Within a year, I had a whole network of Westside families that I worked with."

"Do you like the work?" Jessie asked, looking deeply into the young woman's eyes.

"I do," Robertson said without hesitation. "I work almost exclusively with younger children, kindergarten to fifth grade—that's the age group I want to eventually teach. It's really rewarding to help these kids when they're just starting to grasp concepts. I feel like I'm making a real difference. And I'll admit that the pay is good too."

"What subjects do you teach?" Jessie continued to probe.

"Pretty much everything: reading, writing, math."

"Science?" Ryan wondered pointedly.

"Sure," Robertson said. "But I mean, this is all general knowledge stuff. We're not doing calculus or physics or anything like that. There's a reason I want to teach younger grades. I'm not exactly a whiz in those STEM subjects once we get past the basics. Can I ask you a question, if that's not inappropriate?"

"Of course," Jessie told her.

"You're the police and you're in my apartment," she noted. "You said you had some questions about my clients, but you haven't asked anything about them yet. I'm starting to get worried that something is majorly wrong."

They had delayed the inevitable as long as they could, hoping to glean as much information as they could about Robertson before the dynamic inevitably changed. Jessie looked over at Ryan slightly, letting him know that she was ready if he was. He picked up on it and fixed his attention on the tutor.

"Your clients include Clarissa Langley, Tabitha Reynolds, and Naomi Hacket, correct?" he asked.

"I like to think that their kids are my clients," she replied with a sheepish smile, "but yes. Why?"

"All three of them have been murdered in the last forty-eight hours," he said bluntly.

Robertson, who had been playing with a strand of her hair, froze in place. Her eyes turned into saucers as her jaw dropped open. It took her a few seconds to find words.

"What?" she finally said.

"They've all been killed, Ms. Robertson," he repeated, "so we're speaking to everyone who had connections to all of them. You're one of those people."

"Um, okay," she said, not seeming to fully process the situation. "Would it be all right if I sat down?"

He nodded that it was, and she shuffled over to her couch. She took a seat, her eyes fixed on her bare feet. Jessie and Ryan followed her but remained standing. Ryan was about to continue when the young woman looked up.

"Are the kids okay?" she asked plaintively.

"They're all fine," Jessie told her. "When is the last time you worked with any of them?"

"I'm sorry," Robertson said, looking flustered. "Normally my memory is pretty good, but everything's just swimming around my head right now. Would it be okay if I consult my phone calendar?"

"Of course," Jessie said.

Robertson pulled out her phone and began scrolling. After reviewing things, she looked up.

"Okay, I last worked with Lansing Langley this last Monday, the 19th," she said, her voice less tenuous now that she was focused on her area of expertise.

"But don't most kids have winter break this week?" Jessie asked, perplexed.

Robertson sighed heavily before replying.

"That's true," she said, "but a lot of these parents are pretty intense. They want to take advantage of every opportunity for their children. They view any setback as putting their child at risk of not getting into their preferred college. Lansing got a bad grade on his last math test before break, and Mrs. Langley wanted me to drill him on the concepts."

"How old is he?" Ryan asked.

"He's seven," Robertson replied, wincing. "He knew the material. He just gets nervous taking tests. I told Mrs. Langley that he'd be better off talking to someone about his anxiety than doing math problems over the holidays, but she felt differently."

"What about Tabitha Reynolds?" Jessie asked.

"I work with her daughter, Samantha—Sammy," Robertson said. "I helped her last Thursday because she had a spelling test on Friday. I was actually planning to text Tabitha to see how it went, but I didn't want to bother her over the holidays."

"And what about Naomi Hackett?" Ryan asked. "When did you last work with her child?"

"I saw Olivia—she's five—last Wednesday. She didn't have any tests to study for or anything. She's only in kindergarten, but Naomi thought it might be good to review the material from the last month or so, just to prevent any learning loss over the holidays." Robertson suddenly gasped as she seemed to come to some realization. "Oh my god, I can't believe that little girl is without her mother now."

"Ms. Robertson," Jessie said, not allowing herself to get sucked into that spiral of thoughts for fear it would overwhelm her. After all, this was a murder suspect, and she needed to view her as such.

"You can call me Danielle," the tutor interrupted.

"Danielle," Jessie said, "when you worked with Olivia, was that at the Hackett's home in Pacific Palisades or Naomi's apartment in Playa Vista?"

Danielle looked at her, confused for a second.

"I don't know what you mean," she said, "I only ever went to their house. She has a place in Playa too?"

"You didn't know that?" Jessie asked.

"No," she said. "Nothing like that ever came up. I know she runs—ran—a tech company in the Silicon Beach area, but I didn't know she had a place there too."

Jessie felt her heart sink at that answer. Ryan must have sensed her deflate because he took over.

"She stayed there some weeknights rather than commute home," Ryan told her.

"I guess that would explain why she wasn't around most times I visited Olivia."

"So you've never been to her apartment, even to pick up a check?" Jessie pressed, hoping to find some way to keep this lead alive. "It's not that far from here."

"I wouldn't even know where it is," Danielle explained, "and most of my clients pay via Venmo, Zelle, or PayPal anyway. In a lot of cases, with nannies around, me doing tutoring mostly in the afternoons, and parents working late at high-powered jobs, I'll go weeks or even months without ever seeing them. In fact, in some instances, I've never spoken to the client in person other than during our initial hiring meeting."

Jessie forced herself to keep her disappointment to herself as she responded.

"Would you be willing to let us review the GPS data from your phone and vehicle to confirm what you've told us?" she asked, more out of obligation than anything.

"Of course," Danielle said. "I know you have to verify what I'm saying. I just wish there was something more I could do."

"Maybe there is," Ryan suggested. "Did you notice anything unusual when you were at any of their homes? Interpersonal conflicts? Or something as straightforward as other service providers like yourself who worked for all three women."

Danielle thought for a second. Even before she replied, Jessie could tell from her expression that whatever she had to share would be of little use.

"Like I said, most of the time, the parents weren't around," she explained. "It was just me and the kids, so it's not like I observed any fights or anything like that. As far as providers go, there were people in and out of those homes all the time. I always heard doorbells ringing and voices in other rooms."

"You never saw these people?" Jessie questioned skeptically.

"Hardly ever," Danielle replied. "I would usually work with the child as far from all those distractions as I could, either in their rooms or somewhere else secluded. Even at Tabitha Reynolds's, which was a loft apartment, we worked in Samantha's curtained-off space and Tabitha's housekeeper would deal with anyone who came by. No faces or names jump out at me right now. Still, I could try to go back through my appointments and see if that jogs my memory about anyone who I saw at all of their homes. It might take a while, though. Could I get back to you on that?"

“Sure,” Ryan said, handing over Jamil’s business card. “Call our head of research with what you remember. He’ll also send you a waiver to access your GPS data, so we don’t have to get a court order.”

He indicated to Jessie that they should head out. She followed behind him, trying to keep her frustration hidden and sensing that she was failing. Though Danielle Robertson could still end up being their killer, just like the personal trainer Landon Powers could, what they’d learned here wasn’t promising.

If Danielle’s story held up, she likely wouldn’t have had enough personal interaction to develop a motive for killing them. And if it was true that she’d never even been to Naomi Hackett’s apartment, planting a canister full of poison there was hard to explain.

As they walked out of the apartment and back to the car, Ryan kept silent. He was wise to do so. He knew better than to engage her when she was in this kind of mood. Barring a surprise, their two strongest suspects were dead ends.

Jessie wasn’t sure if she was more depressed or pissed. Either way, they were back to square one, which meant their killer was that much closer to finding another victim. They could be out there right now, hunting for one. Or worse, they might have already found one.

CHAPTER SIXTEEN

Avery Sinclair was dying.

She'd been wearing four inch heels all morning and her calves were screaming at her. So when she finally got home to her Pacific Palisades home, after visiting four properties she'd recently put on the market, she was happy to slip out of those shoes and into some slippers.

It was a temporary reprieve. After having a quick bite for lunch, she had two other couples to meet with, both of whom wanted to list their places early in the new year. The only good thing was that the commute would be negligible, as they each lived nearby, in mansions even more impressive than Avery's own home.

She was just prepping her salad when the doorbell rang. She wasn't in the mood to walk all the way to the front door, so she checked her Ring app to see who it was. Unfortunately, it looked like the thing was acting up again, as the image was fuzzy at best.

The bell rang again, and she reluctantly went to answer it. The gardener, who wasn't supposed to be here until this afternoon, occasionally showed up early. And even though he had a key to the side gate, he wouldn't go in the backyard unless he knew someone was around to authorize it. He'd explained that a neighbor once called the police on him when he was working at a house. Since then, he never took a chance.

Avery looked through the front door peephole and saw that it wasn't the gardener at all. Surprised, she opened the door.

"Hi," she said, trying to be pleasant despite her mild irritation. "I thought we weren't meeting up until after the new year."

"I know," her visitor said. "I'm sorry to just stop by. But I was in the area and thought it might be worth checking in, just in case."

"I would have thought you'd call or text first," Avery said, aware that she was being ungracious but not caring that much. Her salad time was quickly evaporating.

"I actually lost my phone," her visitor said. "Truthfully, I think it might have been stolen, though I can't prove that. That's another reason I figured I'd come by. Until I get a new one later today, I don't know who's been trying to get in touch with me. But if this is a bad time, I can always come back."

Avery didn't like the idea of having to go through all this again soon, so she decided to bite the bullet.

"No, come on in," she said. "But we're going to have to multi-task. I have some appointments soon, so I'm putting together some lunch. We can talk in the kitchen. Close the door behind you."

"Actually," the visitor said as they closed the door, "do you mind if I use your bathroom really quick? I've had to go for a while."

Avery stifled a sigh of frustration and pointed down the hall. "It's the second door on the left," she said. "Just come back this way when you're done. The kitchen is down on the right."

The visitor nodded and headed down the hall. Avery returned to the kitchen and was just starting to chop some carrots when she heard a familiar sound. It was the creak that the stairs made as someone reached the step at the halfway point. Her heart began beating rapidly.

Other than her and the visitor, there wasn't supposed to be anyone in the house right now. Willem was at work. The kids were at her sister's house for the day. The maid had Fridays off. Could the visitor be sneaking upstairs for some reason? That seemed unlikely. Then another thought occurred to Avery. She hadn't been paying close attention earlier. Had the visitor thought to lock the front door after closing it? Had they even closed it all the way? If not, someone on the street might have seen and come in.

Avery clutched the chef's knife she'd been using on the carrots and headed back down the hallway. Her phone was in her pocket, and she was tempted to call 911. But that seemed a little rash. She started down the hallway leading to the bathroom. She could hear the water running and saw the light on under the door.

That only freaked Avery out more. If the visitor was still in the bathroom, that meant that someone else was definitely in the house. She reached the stairs and started up, making sure to skip the creaky step. When she reached the top, she paused and listened closely.

There wasn't any sound, but then she saw it. A shadow appeared in the hallway just outside her bedroom. The light from the window must have cast it. Now certain she had an intruder in the house, she pulled out her phone and dialed 911. She immediately got an automated message telling her someone would be on the line soon. She was inclined to just head back downstairs when she heard a clanking sound.

Then she remembered that after last night's Westside Realtor Awards gala, she'd been so tired that she'd just taken off her diamond tennis necklace and emerald earrings, leaving them on her makeup vanity rather than returning them to the safe. She couldn't risk those being stolen. Together, they were worth close to $15,000.

She shoved her phone back in her pocket and dashed down the hall. As she entered the bedroom, she was stunned and confused by what she saw. The visitor that she'd invited into her home was standing by a bookshelf. They'd moved her "realtor of the year" trophy to the side and were putting some kind of small, metal canister behind a large, framed family photo. But even more shocking, they seemed to be wearing some kind of gas mask.

"What the hell?" Avery demanded, holding the knife out in front of her as she started in that direction.

The visitor turned around, startled, and bumped the bookshelf. The canister fell to the hardwood floor just as Avery arrived. She was debating whether to actually use the knife on the intruder when the canister suddenly beeped and began emitting a hissing sound. Avery looked down at it in confusion.

"What is that?" she barked, looking back up at the visitor just in time to see that they had grabbed her realtor trophy and were swinging the marble base at her head. She threw her hands up to protect herself, but she was too late. The edge of the trophy base smashed into her forehead just above the left temple.

Avery felt a shock of unimaginable pain in her skull as her legs gave out. Her vision was clouded by swimming colors. She felt her body slam to the floor hard, but that pain was nothing compared to the one in her head.

She groaned as she tried to orient herself and look up. Her vision had cleared slightly, but now the colors were replaced by what she assumed was blood seeping into her eyes from her wound. The visitor was standing above her, clutching her trophy tightly.

"This isn't how I wanted it to go," they said, almost apologetically, their voice muffled by the gas mask.

"Please," Avery managed to mutter, though she couldn't think of the rest of the words she should say.

The visitor lifted the trophy high in the air, and it was clear that they intended to use it again. Just before they brought it down, Avery heard a voice on the phone in her pocket.

"911. What is the location of your emergency?"

She wanted to respond, but all she could see was the base of the trophy coming toward her. Then she saw nothing.

CHAPTER SEVENTEEN

Jessie could barely bring herself to eat.

She and Ryan were taking a lunch break at a café in Marina del Rey. The plan had been to review all the leads they had in order to determine who to speak to next, but it had been a slog.

They'd gotten an update from Dr. Roone, but it had only confirmed his initial suspicions. Like Clarissa Langley, both Tabitha Reynolds and Naomi Hackett had died from massive exposure to botulinum toxin.

Jamil and Beth were working on getting the GPS location data for both Danielle Robertson and Landon Powers, but it would take a few hours. Jessie wasn't optimistic that either would pan out, but they didn't have much else to go on.

Despite Parker's insistence that they continue to pursue the professional connection between Clarissa Langley's marketing firm and Naomi Hackett's tech startup, they still hadn't uncovered anything that could tie it to Tabitha Reynolds. She had been so successful promoting herself on social media that she'd never employed any marketing firm, much less Langley's. And her work had no connection at all to Hackett's startup. The rest of the news was no better.

"Even after looking at the video camera footage from each home in more detail," Jamil said, "we weren't able to find anything useful. No one entering or leaving was seen holding a canister and since the devices could have been planted so far in advance, drawing conclusions about more recent visitors is almost pointless anyway."

Beth managed to offer them one mildly intriguing tidbit.

"When Danielle Robertson reached out to authorize us accessing her GPS data, she did mention a few people that she thought she recalled at multiple houses," she told them over speaker. "One was a realtor, and another was a gardener, but she didn't remember any names. She did say that they were both male and that she might be able to identify faces if we showed them to her."

"These people were at all three homes?" Ryan asked.

"No," Jamil said. "That's why we haven't prioritized it. She said she couldn't remember if they were even at more than one home."

"Honestly, she seemed to be grasping at straws," Beth added. "I think she was just hoping to offer anything that might help, no matter how uncertain the leads."

"Still," Jamil assured them, "we're going to go through family financials, looking for any realtors or gardeners that more than one of them used."

Jessie was about to reply when she heard a commotion on the other end of the line. Then Parker's voice came through loud and clear.

"Are you on with Hernandez and Hunt?" she asked the researchers.

"Yes, Captain," Jamil told her. "We're on speaker with them."

"Hi, Captain," Ryan said, sounding surprisingly pleasant. "What's up."

"Nothing good," Parker replied, not matching his tone. "I just got word. There's been another murder, and they just discovered a canister by the body."

"Where was this?" Ryan asked, putting down his sandwich.

"Pacific Palisades," Parker told him. "But this one's different. It looks like the poison didn't have time to work. The victim's head was crushed in."

"Send us whatever you have," Jessie said, grabbing her mostly untouched turkey wrap as she stood up. "We're leaving now."

***

Twenty five minutes later, they arrived at the home of Avery Sinclair.

On the way over, they'd gotten the basics on the woman from the research team. She was 41, married, with two children. She worked as a realtor. In fact, according to Jamil, she was this year's Westside Realtor of the Year. Jessie looked over photos of the woman, including from her website. She was strikingly beautiful, statuesque, with long red hair, green eyes, ivory skin, and delicate, angular facial features.

Jessie looked up from her phone screen as they arrived on Sinclair's street. They could identify her house by the multiple vehicles in front of it, which included a hazmat vehicle, a fire truck, three police cars, an ambulance, as well as vehicles from CSU and the coroner. They were just getting out of the car when they were approached by a tall officer with curly brown hair that Jessie didn't know.

"Hi," he said, waving as he approached, "I'm Sergeant Watt, lead officer on the scene. I recognized you when you were pulling up."

They introduced themselves before Ryan launched in. “Let me guess. The hazmat team has sealed off the house. No investigators are allowed in yet.”

"That's right," Watt told them. "No one but them is permitted inside until they clear the scene. Unfortunately, the first officers to arrive have already been transported to the hospital."

“Are they okay?” Jessie asked.

“Neither of them showed any obvious signs of being affected but they were transported to UCLA Santa Monica Medical Center anyway as a precaution,” Watt answered.

“How did your people originally learn about the incident?” Jessie asked.

"The first officers on the scene were responding to a 911 call," Watt explained. "The operator said it sounded over the phone like someone was being assaulted. When they arrived, it was eight minutes after the call to 911, which occurred at 12:06 p.m. No one answered the door, so they forced entry. After a quick search, they found the victim in her bedroom. They called for backup and took some preliminary photos, including of the victim and the murder weapon, which appears to have been a trophy."

“When did the hazmat team get involved?” Ryan asked.

“After their initial inspection of the scene, one of the responding officers noticed a metal canister partially hidden under the bed,” Watt told them. “That immediately raised alarm bells. Everyone knows about the recent spate of poison killings and has seen what those canisters look like. The moment they saw this one, they evacuated and called for the hazmat team.”

“Were they able to send you the photos they took?” Jessie asked, feeling slightly guilty for sounding like that was a greater concern to her than the officers’ welfare.

“They were,” Watt said, unfazed. “I have them here and can forward them to you as well.”

He held out his phone. The first image was of the trophy. That was blood and hair on the marble base of it. The second photo was a wide shot of Avery Sinclair lying on her bedroom floor. Blood had pooled around her head.

The third photo was a close-up of her wounds. Even with all her experience, it was hard for Jessie to take. Maybe what she saw was made worse by the images she’d just seen of Sinclair looking so put together on her realty website bio page. But the woman in the photo was unrecognizable.

The killer had struck at least four blows to separate parts of her head. Her face was covered in blood and there were deep indentations in the top of her skull, her forehead, her cheekbone, and an eye socket. Jessie looked away, trying not to think about the two young children who would learn later today that their mommy was gone and not coming back.

"Did the hazmat team provide an estimate for when we might be able to get in there?" Ryan asked.

"Nothing firm," Watt replied, "but if you give me a minute, I can try to get an update."

"That would be great," Ryan told him.

Watt dashed off in the direction of the house. When he was out of earshot, Ryan said what Jessie had been thinking.

"What was the point of even coming all this way?" he growled in frustration. "If the hazmat team isn't going to let us in anytime soon, we're just spinning our wheels. We could have looked at those photos back in Marina del Rey."

Jessie couldn't disagree and was about to say so when their phones rang. It was the number for research. Jessie put the call on speaker.

"Please tell us you have something," she pleaded.

"Nothing hugely promising," Beth answered. "We're still in the preliminary stages of looking for shared connections between Sinclair and the other victims, but so far we're coming up empty."

"What have you checked?" Ryan asked.

"Since Sinclair had two children," Beth continued, "we looked to see if she was using Danielle Robertson as a tutor, but based on an initial review of her finances, it doesn't appear that she used any tutor at all for them."

"What about Landon Powers?" Jessie wondered. "Any sign that she ever used him as a trainer."

"Not that we can find so far," Beth answered. "She belongs to a gym, but not the one Powers is based out of and her personal trainer is a woman."

Jessie couldn't help but sigh. Both she and Ryan were quiet for a moment before she realized that the other researcher hadn't said anything.

"Has Jamil found anything?" she asked.

"He's looking into another lead right now, but so far, it hasn't gone anywhere."

Sergeant Watt was jogging back over. Jessie could tell from his expression that the news wasn't good.

"The hazmat team tells me it will be at least another hour before they can authorize entry into the home, probably two before anyone can get up to the bedroom."

Jessie was about to express her dissatisfaction verbally when she was interrupted by Jamil's voice.

"Excuse me," he said over speaker, his tone suggesting he was excited about what he was about to share.

"Go ahead," Jessie told him, trying not to get her hopes up.

"I was following up on a hunch," he said. "When I learned that Avery Sinclair was a realtor, it made me think back to how Danielle Robertson mentioned a realtor coming by at least one of the other victims' homes. I noted that when Sinclair won realtor of the year, the runner-up was a guy named Mitchell Vaughn, Jr.. The name sounded familiar, so I just cross-checked it."

Jessie felt a tingle in her fingers as she listened, sensing that something significant was about to be revealed. She stayed quiet as Jamil continued.

"It turns out that he was involved with at least two of the other victims. When Tabitha Reynolds and her husband got divorced, Vaughn was the realtor when they sold their home. And when Naomi Hackett's family moved down here from the Bay Area, he was the realtor for the family they bought their house from."

"That's great work," Ryan exclaimed. "Any link to Clarissa Langley?"

"Not that I could find so far," Jamil conceded.

"There's got to be something," Jessie insisted. "This feels right. I mean, the woman was killed with the very trophy that she won, proving that she bested him. If it *was* him, it must have felt like poetic justice to use it as the murder weapon."

"Actually," Beth volunteered, "when I was looking through the Langley's financials before, I saw that they paid for staging services for their home earlier this year. There was nothing about them putting the place on the market, but maybe they were considering it and changed their mind. If that's the case, they would have surely met with some realtors to discuss it."

Jessie looked at Ryan and said what she knew he was thinking.

"Let's go find out!"

CHAPTER EIGHTEEN

By the time they pulled up at Mitchell Vaughn's Santa Monica realty office fifteen minutes later, they knew a lot more, and none of it reflected well on the guy.

It turned out that Vaughn, 40, was fairly notorious for his aggressive tactics in the Westside realty world. He'd filed over three dozen complaints against other realtors in his career, including seven just this year. Two of those complaints were against Avery Sinclair.

In response she'd actually filed a restraining order against him with the LAPD, claiming that he constantly harassed her online, over the phone, and in-person, even coming to her house once to berate her from the other side of her closed front door.

And she wasn't the only one. Three other women had filed restraining orders against him in the last decade, all claiming similar behavior on his part. One of the instances, three years ago, led to a criminal charges being filed.

The statement from the woman in that case, whom he had briefly dated, mentioned erratic behavior on his part, including putting his clothes in a pile in her front yard and burning them. In that instance, he pleaded no contest to a misdemeanor and got six months' probation and a fine.

"It seems like we've got a real winner," Ryan said in disgust after Jessie finished reciting the litany of incidences Jamil had sent them. "I guess we're about to find out if he's escalated to a new level."

They entered the office, which was in a surprisingly run-down storefront that shared the block with a liquor store and a donut shop. The receptionist, a weary-looking woman in her fifties with gray hair and bifocals, looked up as they walked in. A nameplate on her desk read: *Marian Voytek.*

"We're looking for Mitchell Vaughn, Jr.," Ryan said sharply, flashing his badge.

Marian's expression suggested that she wasn't shocked to have police showing up asking questions about her boss, and she simply pointed at a closed door at the end of a short hallway. Ryan nodded in thanks and marched ahead. Jessie trotted to catch up.

With one hand on his gun holster, Ryan opened the door and barged in unannounced. The man, sitting behind a rickety-looking desk, jumped in his seat. Vaughn's attire was a significant upgrade from his office. Dressed in an expensive suit, his dark hair was perfectly styled and popped against his suspiciously tan skin. The man, even startled, was attractive, though his brown eyes were red and droopy.

After his moment of confusion, Vaughn shot up angrily. He was easily six foot two and while he wasn't muscularly built as Ryan, he looked like he could be formidable when riled up.

"Who in the hell do you think—?" he started to bark before Ryan cut him off.

"Detective Ryan Hernandez, LAPD," he growled, holding out his badge. "We've got a few questions for you, Mr. Vaughn, and unless we like the answers you give us, today is going to go very badly for you."

Even though Jessie understood where her husband's anger was coming from—she shared it—she didn't love the aggression that he was starting off with. She'd seen the horrific photos of Avery Sinclair's head, too, but this tactic didn't leave them anywhere to go. Unfortunately what was done was done so she did her best to hide the disapproving grimace she felt forming at her lips.

"I'm sorry," Vaughn retorted belligerently. "I didn't know that it was the LAPD's job to burst into a working man's office and start making demands. How about you give me the respect I deserve in my own place of business?"

Rather than feeling cowed, the guy was vibrating with fury of his own. Things were escalating far too quickly. At this rate, someone was going to get hurt before they got any answers.

"Mr. Vaughn," she said calmly. "I'm Jessie Hunt. I work with Detective Hernandez. We're dealing with a very volatile situation, otherwise we wouldn't come into your office like this. But we need you to stand down and answer our questions. It's an important matter and being combative won't do anyone any good."

"Talk to your partner there about being combative!" Vaughn shouted, pointing at Ryan, before suddenly freezing. He turned to look at Jessie more closely. "What did you say your name was again?"

"Jessie Hunt," she answered, getting a sinking feeling.

"I know that name," he said. "You're that profiler who hunts serial killers."

"That's correct," she replied, waiting for what she now knew was inevitable.

“If you’re here, then that means something terrible has happened,” he told her, “and the way your pal is acting, it feels like you want to pin it on me. So I’m not saying a damn word.”

“Mr. Vaughn,” she said. “We are here about a very serious matter. But this is your opportunity to prove to us that you’re *not* involved. We can clear up any confusion right here and now. But if you’re not willing to talk, you’re probably going to get arrested. I know we all want to avoid that.”

He looked at her closely, apparently sizing up whether she was bluffing or not. Then he looked over at Ryan, who still had one hand on his badge and another on his holster. In that moment, he seemed to make his decision.

“I have just one word for you,” he said, his mouth turning into a nasty, twisted grin.

“What’s that?” she asked though she already knew the answer and how difficult it would make solving this case.

“Lawyer.”

CHAPTER NINETEEN

Jessie seethed quietly.

She and Ryan were waiting in a conference room at the West Los Angeles police station, where they'd taken Mitchell Vaughn. They'd agreed that it made more sense to try to interrogate him there rather than drive all the way back downtown to Central Station. After all, if they could somehow eliminate Vaughn as a suspect, at least they'd be in the right part of town to continue to investigate.

But it turned out that there was no interrogation, which is what had Jessie so furious. After Vaughn had invoked his right to a lawyer back at his office, Ryan had read him his rights. But once that formality was complete, Jessie had tried to get the guy to change his mind.

Both in the car on the way over and in the interrogation room where they'd placed him, she did her best to cajole him into cooperating. Since she wasn't a cop, it wasn't technically a violation for her to continue to question Vaughn, although it came close to the line.

It didn't matter. The realtor didn't say a word the whole drive to the station. After a few minutes in the interrogation room of Jessie trying to re-establish a connection with him in order to get him chatting, he finally stared her in the eyes.

"Two words this time," he said slowly. "Lawyer, bitch."

She left the interrogation room without speaking. Ryan, who had calmed down since his outburst at the office, made the call. It turned out that Vaughn had a personal criminal attorney, which made sense, as he seemed to need one often.

"The lawyer is on his way," Ryan said, sounding somewhat chastened as he joined her in the conference room. "He reminded us not to speak to his client until he arrived."

"Funny how that works," Jessie grumbled. "I guess when you try to intimidate a guy who has experience with the criminal justice system, rather than take a more accommodating approach, he tends to shut down and give you nothing."

"I know I made a mistake," Ryan said quietly. "I let my frustration get the better of me. Between Captain Parker pressing us all the time and seeing what was done to Avery Sinclair, I guess I lost my grip a little."

Jessie turned to face him directly when she replied.

"I get it," she said. "I feel these losses more than anyone. Don't forget that I lost my mother to a murderer—my own father—when I was just six. Seeing all these young kids lose theirs is gutting me. But you're the seasoned professional here. If anyone is supposed to rein in spiraling emotions, it should be you doing that to me. Now we can't get anything out of this guy."

A knock on the conference room door made them both look up. A young, brown-haired female officer named Stoller poked her head in.

"The receptionist for Mitchell Vaughn is here. She said you wanted her to come in for an interview."

"Thanks," Ryan said, "Please send her in."

A minute later, Officer Stoller brought Marian Voytek back. Ryan motioned for her to have a seat opposite them. She looked significantly more nervous now than she had back at the realty office.

"Thanks for coming in, Ms. Voytek," Ryan began.

"You can call me Marian," she told him.

"How long have you worked for Mitchell Vaughn, Marian?" Jessie asked.

"About four years now," the woman answered.

"Are you very involved in his work?" Jessie continued. "Do you know his clients?"

"I didn't meet any of them personally," Marian said. "I usually stay in the office and Mitch liked to meet with clients in the field."

"Do you recognize the names Tabitha Reynolds or Naomi Hackett?" Ryan asked.

"Sure," Marian replied immediately. "Vaughn Realty was the selling agency on the Reynolds home and on the home that the Hacketts bought."

"What about Clarissa Langley?" Ryan wondered.

Marian scrunched up her brow at that question, trying to recall.

"That name doesn't immediately ring a bell," she conceded, "which makes me think we never officially had her as a client. But that doesn't mean she didn't meet with Mitch at some point. I keep records of all meetings in our office files, so if there was any engagement, it would be in there."

"We might have someone accompany you back to the office to look into that momentarily," Ryan told her.

"Of course," Marian said, then hesitated briefly before adding, "Can I ask what this is about?"

"Mitch is a suspect in four murders," Jessie said flatly, watching Marian's response closely. "Does that surprise you?"

The way the woman's eyes widened suggested that it did.

"I mean, he's definitely had some legal issues, but nothing like that. When you guys first came into the office earlier, I thought it was going to be related to gambling stuff."

"What do you mean?" Ryan asked.

Marian offered a wry smile.

"Why do you think that his office is so run down?" she asked. "We used to have space in an upscale shopping plaza in Brentwood. But Mitch started paring everything down lately. The only things he spends money on now are his personal look and his car—so clients are impressed—and the games he bets on."

"You're saying he has a problem?" Jessie asked.

"Only if you consider being $120,000 in debt a problem," Marian replied. "Why do you think the guy is so aggressive in targeting other realtors? Why has he had multiple harassment incidents and restraining orders? He's under constant pressure to secure as many clients and make as many home sales as possible."

"I'm assuming these aren't legitimate bookmakers?" Ryan said.

"He's never told me that specifically," Marian, "but in the last six months, he's 'broken' both pinkie fingers and 'lost' a tooth. So you tell me. To be honest, when you said you were a cop, I thought you might have come to arrest him for robbing a bank or something."

Jessie sighed. Vaughn obviously had serious issues, but it wasn't clear to her how they might be connected to Avery Sinclair's murder.

"Do you know where he was today around noon?" she asked.

"Yeah," Marian said, "he came into the office late. I think he might have gone on a bit of a bender last night. There was this big realty awards gala and I saw that he lost on the big award to Avery Sinclair. He considers her his nemesis, if you can believe it. When I saw that news, I knew he'd take it hard and that today would be ugly. So I wasn't stunned when he didn't show up until lunchtime. I didn't bother calling him to check in. When he finally arrived, he walked straight back to his office without a word and slammed the door. I think he might have been napping when you got here. You probably woke him up."

"What time was that?" Ryan asked.

"12:19."

"Are you sure?" Jessie pressed. "That's so specific."

"Yeah, I'm positive," Marian said.

"How?" Jessie asked.

"Because when he slammed the door, the clock on the wall fell and broke. The time read 12:19, so I have a permanent reminder of when he came in today."

Jessie shared a look with Ryan and saw that he was making the same calculation that she was. It had taken them fifteen minutes to get from Sinclair's Pacific Palisades mansion to Vaughn's Santa Monica office and they weren't driving slow. They knew that Sinclair's 911 call occurred at 12:06 p.m. And according to Marian, Vaughn arrived at his office at 12:19.

That meant that he would have had to beat Avery Sinclair to death, go downstairs, get out of her house, into his car, and drive to his office in thirteen minutes. That was an incredibly tight window, if not technically impossible.

"We should check in with the team that impounded his car," Ryan said. "If he did this, he wouldn't have much time to clean up. Maybe there's blood splatter in the vehicle."

"Or possibly a gas mask," Jessie added. "If he was planting a poison canister in Sinclair's home, he would have probably wanted to take precautions. Hell, maybe there's a canister in the trunk."

"Wait," Marian interrupted. "Are you saying that Avery Sinclair is dead?"

"She is," Ryan replied.

"And you think that Mitch killed her? Using some kind of poison?"

"That's not how it ended up playing out," Jessie said, "but we think that was the original plan. You sound skeptical."

Marian shook her head in disbelief.

"It's just that poisoning someone, wearing a gas mask? That stuff's not really in Mitch's wheelhouse. He's good at sales. But chemicals? Knowing him for four years now, I can say that the guy isn't exactly a science person."

"Well, people can be surprising," Jessie noted, though she was inclined to trust Marian's assessment. "In any case, we're going to have an officer accompany you back to the realty office so you can search the files for anything related to Clarissa Langley. Thanks for your time. I'll see you out."

She walked the woman back to reception and assigned Officer Stoller to accompany her to the office. After giving Stoller instructions on what to do once they got there, she returned to the conference room, where she saw that Ryan's brow was furrowed.

"What is it?" she asked.

"I checked with the vehicle impound team," he said. "They have to get Vaughn's car back to the station for a comprehensive review. But upon their initial search, they didn't find any obvious signs of blood. No gas masks or poison canisters showed up either."

"Maybe he got lucky on the blood," Jessie suggested unenthusiastically, "and he could have tossed those other things in a dumpster on the way into the office."

Ryan looked at her skeptically.

"Do you believe that?" he asked.

"It would make an already tight window to get back to the office even smaller," she conceded, "and I've been thinking about what Marian said. Mitchell Vaughn doesn't seem to have the meticulous personality required to pull off the first three murders, even if this last one, which was more about brute force, seems like something he could handle."

They both sat silently at the conference room table, pondering all the permutations in front of them. The quiet was interrupted by a call on Ryan's phone. He glanced down at it.

"Parker," he said without enthusiasm. "Maybe I let it go to voicemail?"

Jessie shook her head.

"Answer it," she said. "She's our station captain and she deserves an update, even if she's not going to like it."

Ryan sighed heavily and hit "accept."

"Hi, Captain," he said, hiding his feelings well. "How are you?"

"Impatient, Detective Hernandez," she told him. "I understand that you made an arrest, but I haven't heard anything from you. Everything I know of late comes from your research team. Can I impose on you to share the status of your case?"

"Sorry," he replied convincingly. "We've been 'go go go' for the last hour. Here's what we know so far. The suspect we have in custody is Mitchell Vaughn Jr., a real estate agent in the area—."

"Actually," Parker interrupted, "Jamil and Beth already updated me, so things might go faster if I tell you what I already know, and you fill in what's missing."

"Okay," Ryan replied, trying to maintain his cool.

"My understanding is that you were able to connect him to two victims through home sales," Parker said. "In addition, Avery Sinclair filed a restraining order against him. He also appears to have had a personal vendetta against Sinclair that was exacerbated by some realtor award ceremony just last night, is that correct?"

"Yes, Captain," Ryan confirmed.

"And I'm told that the murder weapon was the very trophy that Sinclair won at his expense."

"Also true," Ryan said.

"That seems compelling," she noted drily. "Any connection to Clarissa Langley yet?"

"Not yet," he said, "but we're checking his office files to see if we can find one."

Jessie didn't volunteer the tidbit that had Ryan not come on so strong with Vaughn they might already know if there was a connection.

"Well, even without that, it seems that we have more than enough for the D.A. to file charges," Parker said. "You can understand why I'm surprised that I haven't heard anything from you to that effect."

"Captain, if I may," Jessie piped in for the first time, "we feel that might be premature at this point."

"Really?" Parker asked, sounding truly shocked. "I can't wait to hear why, Ms. Hunt."

"First," Jessie said, not loving the disdain she heard, "As Detective Hernandez said, we have yet to establish a connection between Vaughn and Clarissa Langley. Without one, the rest of the case could crumble."

"But your people investigating his files could find one at any time, yes?" Parker prodded.

"They could," Jessie conceded, "but that hasn't happened yet. In addition, the window of time for Vaughn to have committed this crime and returned to his office, where an eyewitness confirmed his presence, is very brief."

"Too brief to have done it?"

"No," Jessie said. "But it would have been especially challenging without any stops along the way. And we understand that no gas mask was found in his car, which suggests he would have had to dump that en route to his office, adding even more time to the trip."

"What makes you so certain that he had a gas mask?"

"I can't be certain," Jessie acknowledged, "but this chemical is extremely volatile, and the killer knows that better than anyone. The idea that they handled it without protection seems very unlikely."

"But not impossible," Parker noted, unmoved. "Any other reason I shouldn't tell Chief Decker that he can hold a news conference saying we've got our guy? I know he's wanted to get that out by the 5 p.m. local news."

"Yes, Captain," Jessie said, feeling like a salmon swimming upstream. "We haven't gotten prints back from the trophy that was used to kill Avery Sinclair. They might definitively identify the killer."

Even as she said it, Jessie knew this wasn't her strongest argument. Ryan's wince validated her concern. And sure enough, Parker pounced.

"Ms. Hunt, are you telling me that our killer had the foresight and wherewithal to plant timer-based, motion-activated poison-filled canisters inside the homes of three woman without being captured on surveillance video or leaving any other trace of usable evidence at the scenes, including zero prints on those canisters, but in this one instance, they forgot to wear gloves? How likely does that sound?"

"Not very," Jessie admitted, "but this murder was different than the others. I believe Sinclair surprised the killer while they were planting the canister, leading to the bludgeoning. Maybe the murderer removed their gloves at some point. Maybe Sinclair was able to pull one off in a struggle. What's the harm in waiting a few hours for more firm results?"

"The harm is that there is a city full of scared people out there who want some sense that they are safe and secure in their own homes," Parker told her. "Unless you can offer something more concrete than 'maybes,' I don't think we've got a strong enough reason to keep all these Angelenos so fearful."

"There's another thing, Captain," Jessie said, hoping a different tactic might make the Parker re-think her position. "Whoever committed these crimes was smart and painstakingly methodical. Mitchell Vaughn is not that. He's a hothead who appears to operate on instinct. He's also a gambler in massive debt to…who knows? He exudes sweaty desperation. It doesn't fit with these murders."

She waited silently, hoping that argument would be compelling. But Parker was undeterred.

"I don't see it, Ms. Hunt," she said impatiently. "It sounds like he simply didn't have as much personal antagonism to the first three victims as he did to the last one, which suggests how he could have been more calculated in prepping their murders. But in Sinclair's case, his animosity may have gotten in the way, clouding his judgment and leading to the trophy attack."

Jessie felt a growing sense of hopelessness. She wasn't entirely sure why she was fighting this so hard. Parker was making powerful counterpoints to everything she brought up. But something just didn't feel quite right about Vaughn.

"Captain," Ryan finally said, sounding cool and collected despite the deteriorating situation, "I don't want to speak for Jessie, but I do know that, like me, she has enormous affection for Chief Decker. He has been incredibly supportive of us both. When I was near death after Jessie's ex-husband attacked me, he was there for me. And last spring, he used every tool at his disposal to help rescue Jessie when she was kidnapped by Andrea Robinson. We love and respect him. And we're just uncomfortable letting him put himself out there, making broad claims on the news that might ultimately come back to bite him and undermine his authority."

Jessie stared at her husband, her heart filled with admiration and love. He had just verbalized exactly what Jessie was feeling but couldn't identify.

"I appreciate that, Detective Hernandez," Parker replied, "But it's actually Chief Decker driving the bus on this one. He wants to give that press briefing, and soon."

"Captain Parker," Jessie pleaded, "if Vaughn is the killer, don't you think that it's a little too obvious for him to have smashed Avery Sinclair's head in with the very trophy she beat him out for the night before? Couldn't someone be turning him into a patsy?"

"Perhaps," Parker conceded, "but you yourself said that he's more of a volatile personality than a meticulous one. Maybe he just lost himself in the moment."

"Maybe," Jessie agreed, "but doesn't that uncertainty earn us a few hours to follow up? It's still only 2:15. Chief Decker could hold his press conference at 4:30 and still have more than enough time to get it on the news. Hell, I bet some stations would carry it live. Please, just give us a couple of hours to follow up on these loose ends."

There was a long pause in which Jessie assumed Parker was pondering the request. But when the silence extended to ten seconds, she thought maybe the call had dropped.

"Captain?" Ryan said.

"I'm sorry," Parker said, her voice heavy with concern. "I was just getting an update from my assistant."

"On the case?" Jessie asked.

"No," Parker said. "Regarding Dr. Janice Lemmon. Officers are at her office. There's been an incident."

Jessie felt her heart stop.

CHAPTER TWENTY

"Is she okay?" Jessie demanded.

"I'm trying to determine that right now," Parker said. "There's a lot of confusion."

"What officer are you talking to?" Ryan asked, wrapping a protective arm around Jessie's shoulder. "Can you conference them in with us?"

Before Parker could reply, Jessie got a call on her cell. The screen read simply: *Lemmon.* She answered it immediately, hoping that the psychiatrist would be on the other end of the line and not some officer bearing bad news.

"Dr. Lemmon?"

"Jessie," the familiar voice of Janice Lemmon said, "I'm okay, mostly."

"What do you mean?" Jessie asked, feeling like a child talking to a parent.

"There was an intruder," Lemmon said. "He attacked me. I was able to fend him off, but not before I got a few bruises and a nasty cut on my forehead. The EMTs are cleaning it up now, but they want to take me to the hospital to suture it properly and do a more thorough work-up on me."

"But you're going to be okay?" Jessie appealed.

"I'm going to be okay," Lemmon assured her.

Jessie was amazed at the woman's calm, almost clinical tone. Admittedly, before she left law enforcement to focus on psychiatry, Janice Lemmon had been a profiler who worked with the FBI and LAPD. She'd seen more awful stuff than most. But to be so composed in the face of an imminent threat to her own safety was remarkable.

"What happened?" Ryan asked.

"It appears that Jessie's old friend, Mark Haddonfield, has long tentacles. Another one of his devotees, who apparently also read his manifesto, decided that as long as people were trying to take out her friends and family, an old lady with a cane might make a good target. I don't know how he found out I was your therapist, Jessie, but he did.

Anyway, he waited until Amy went on her lunch break and I was eating alone in the office."

"I thought you increased your security lately?" Ryan said.

"I did," Lemmon told him, "with additional locks *and* a security guard hired by the building who patrols our floor regularly. But apparently this young man waited until the guard went to the restroom to make his move. He broke into the outer office and then my inner one. Then he charged at me with a hatchet. Luckily, when I heard all the hubbub in the outer office, I had to time to get out the taser I now keep in my top drawer. I fired it at him, and he collapsed. Unfortunately, his momentum led him to collapse into me too, knocking me out of my chair and slashing my head on a cabinet. Thus, the bruises and the impressive gash. The guard heard me calling for help and secured the young man—who was still convulsing from the taser—until the police arrived."

"But the EMTs don't think you have any life-threatening injuries," Jessie said, as if speaking the words forcefully would make it so.

"We'll know for sure in a bit, but I think it will turn out to be just bumps, bruises, and cuts," Lemmon said, before adding, "They're telling me that I have to hang up. They're going to take me down to the ambulance in a stretcher, and we're about to get moving."

"Okay," Ryan said. "Please give us an update when you're able."

"Will do," Lemmon said before hanging up.

In the brief silence that followed, one thought came into Jessie's head. This had to end. How many of the people she cared about would continue to be put at risk in her name? Mitch was dead. Kat had almost met the same fate. And now Dr. Lemmon had barely escaped a hatchet attack in her own office.

Jessie could think of only one way to make this stop. She had to go to the source. Despite everyone's recommendation that she not feed the beast—that it would only make things worse—she had to meet with Mark Haddonfield.

"Are we all still on the line?" Captain Parker asked after what she apparently deemed a respectful pause.

"We are," Ryan told her. "Dr. Lemmon is gone, but Jessie and I are still here."

"I didn't want to interrupt your conversation, but I was glad to hear the doctor seems to be doing okay," Parker said. "I'd certainly understand if you wanted to go to the hospital to see her, Ms. Hunt."

"No," Jessie said quickly. "We all heard her. She sounds like she's in good hands. I'll go check on her when I get a chance. But right now, I want to finish out this case."

"All right," Paker said, her tone softer than it was prior to the call from Lemmon. "Here's what I can offer you: two hours. You have until 4:30 to disprove Mitchell Vaughn as our killer. No later. I'm going to tell Chief Decker he can schedule his news conference for that time. If you don't have anything conclusive by then, he names Vaughn. Fair?"

Jessie didn't know if Parker was making the concession because she had some doubt about Vaughn's guilt or merely out of pity because her psychiatrist had nearly been killed. Either way, she'd take it.

"Fair," she said.

"Thanks, Captain," Ryan added.

"Don't thank me yet," Parker warned. "The clock is ticking. I suggest you get a move on."

Then she hung up. Jessie didn't mind the abruptness this time. They were going to need every second. She had just over two hours to decide if they had a serial killer in custody or if the person poisoning all these women was still out there.

CHAPTER TWENTY ONE

Hank Costabile did his best not to grin.

After weeks of frustration, after endless hiccups, it was finally time. He was going after Jessie Hunt. The moment for action was only seconds away but he made sure that his outward appearance gave no hint of that.

As he sat on a bench outside the Hollywood/Vine Red Line Metro Station, he looked casually at his phone. To anyone walking by, it appeared that he might simply be perusing a news story or checking sports scores. But in fact, he was actually reconfirming the details of the Metro trains. For his plan to work, he had to get this exactly right.

Hank glanced up for a moment to check on the location of his minders. The two plainclothes officers assigned to follow him by police chief Decker were sitting in their gray sedan, parked in front of a palm tree beside the famous Hollywood Walk of Fame sidewalk lined with the names of luminaries past and present. Hank had passed by them earlier and saw that they were right next to the star for Reese Witherspoon.

They made no attempt to hide themselves. It was a silly game they all played. He knew they were watching him, and they knew he knew. When he'd parked his car in an adjoining public lot, they'd idled just outside the gate, waiting to see where he would go next. When he crossed the street to get a burger nearby, they pulled into their current spot. He had lulled them into a sense of complacency. They had no idea what was coming next.

He'd followed this route before on several occasions, just to make himself comfortable, but he'd always done it in a relaxed ambling manner that suggested to his police tail that he was simply enjoying the pleasures of Hollywood. In truth, he was checking the departure times of the trains, making sure they matched the real-time analysis of an app that proudly claimed "99.2% Metro time accuracy- for better commuting!" In his personal experience, the site had been accurate within ten seconds for each route he'd tested. He hoped that didn't change today.

The clock on his phone turned over from 3:26 to 3:27. Hank stood up, nonchalantly balling up the wrapper for his burger and tossing it in a trash bin, before heading over to the giant escalator that led down to the bowels of the Metro station. At the last moment, he veered slightly left and chose the stairs instead. He took the first few steps at a normal pace.

Only when he knew that he was far enough down the stairs that the officers watching him couldn't see the top of his head anymore, did he suddenly pick up the pace. He darted down the steps as quickly as he could, well aware that the officer in the passenger seat of the sedan, who he knew to be a four-year vet of the force named Carrera, would have gotten out of the car by now and have made his way toward the escalators.

Once Officer Carrera reached the top of the stairs, looked down, and saw that Hank was already out of sight, he'd know something was wrong. He'd understand that Hank could only have made it down the stairs that fast if he'd been rushing. And once Officer Carrera knew Hank was rushing, he'd realize that the situation had changed.

That's why, once Hank got to the bottom of the stairs, he broke into a full run. He rounded the corner to the right, sprinted down the long hallway, and then curled left to the turnstiles leading to the platform.

He already had his phone out and swiped it in front of the sensor, waiting the half-second for it to register. The last thing he needed was to jump the turnstile and face off with some chesty security guard intent on giving him a hard time. He wasn't worried about losing a physical altercation. He just couldn't spare the extra seconds.

Once through the turnstile, he dashed down the stairs to the platform, looking around desperately for Willie. Sure enough, the homeless man was exactly where Hank had instructed him to wait, sitting on the wooden bench halfway along the platform behind a pillar. Hank hurried over to him.

As he approached the man, the eastbound train pulled into the station. Hank looked down at his phone. The train was only four seconds late, almost exactly matching the app. While he walked, he took off his green jacket, which he'd intentionally worn today for its boldness, and shoved it into a nearby trash can.

Willie saw him and immediately took off the blue Dodgers cap he was wearing and handed it to Hank, along with a windbreaker and a small backpack that had been sitting on his lap. Hank handed over five

$20 bills, the second half of the payment he'd promised Willie when he first made the deal with him earlier this week.

"Thanks, Willie," Hank muttered quietly as he slid the cap onto his bald head. "A guy should be coming down the stairs in the next few seconds. He has black curly hair and is wearing a brown leather jacket over a blue dress shirt."

"Got it," Willie said.

Next to them, the train came to stop. People began filing out while others waited patiently for their chance to get on.

"Remember he's a cop—don't touch him or try to physically stop him," Hank warned as he put on the blue windbreaker. "Just get in his path and start acting like you know him. Once he gets by you, let him go. Don't make your move for a few seconds. After you do, the rest should fall into place from there."

Willie nodded and headed back in the direction of the platform stairs. As he did, the westbound train arrived at the station, just as it was supposed to. Hank flung the backpack over his shoulder and headed to the open doors of the eastbound train. He fought the urge to look back toward the stairs. By now, Officer Carrera would likely be at the top of them, trying to locate him. Glancing in that direction might give him away.

Once onboard the train, he moved to a spot where he could look out the window without being seen. At that moment, the doors to the westbound train opened. As far as Officer Carrera would know, the man he was after could have hopped on either one.

The stairs were barely in view from his position, but he could make out Willie as he scurried up. At the halfway point, the man stopped and seemed to talk to someone, moving his hands animatedly. A second later, Officer Carrera came into view, looking alarmed at how agitated Willie was, even as he tried to survey the platform for his target.

Hank looked down at his phone again. According to the app, the eastbound train was supposed to pull out in twenty seconds. That meant the door would surely close in the next five to ten. Officer Carrera, only briefly deterred by Willie, brushed by the man and hurried to the bottom of the stairs.

Hank knew exactly what the man was thinking. *Should I get on this train or the westbound one ?Or is Costabile hiding behind a pillar here on the platform, ready to leave this station once the train I get on pulls away.* Then he seemed to decide, stepping toward the doors of Hank's train, which somehow still hadn't closed!

But a moment later, Hank saw Willie tap him on the shoulder. Officer Carrera whirled around, pulling his weapon from his holster at lightning speed. Just then, the train doors hissed and slammed shut.

The last thing Hank saw as the train started to pull away was Willie with his hands in the air and a smile on his face. He'd followed the plan perfectly. Now, the man only had one more thing to do. Hank hoped that even with no more money on the line, he'd complete his final task.

Hank retreated to an empty seat and immediately unzipped the backpack, pulling out a purple Lakers cap and a cheap black rain poncho. He took off the windbreaker and the Dodger cap, stuffed them in the backpack, and changed into the new items.

Then he opened the smaller, front pocket of the backpack, the one with the secret, padded pouch that had led him to purchase this pack in the first place. He pulled the switchblade out of the pouch and slid it into his pocket.

He glanced at the train app again. They would arrive at the next stop, Hollywood & Western, in two minutes. He would get off there, leave the station, dump the backpack in a street-level trash can, and catch a cab—which he would pay for in cash—to his next destination.

Then, he would hole up and wait for the call from the Central Station dispatch sergeant, who would let him know when it was time to make his move. He was almost in the wind. And soon, Jessie Hunt would be in the ground.

CHAPTER TWENTY TWO

Time was running out.

Jessie looked at the clock on the wall of the small conference room. It read: 3:34 p.m. They had less than an hour until Chief Decker's news conference about the poison canister murders, and so far, they had nothing to go on.

It wasn't for a lack of effort. They had checked back in with everyone who could be of help. Sergeant Watt from the Avery Sinclair crime scene had filled them in on what he knew.

"There was a Ring camera on Sinclair's front door, but it wasn't operating properly," he had explained when they spoke earlier. "We checked the footage from just prior to the 911 call, and it looks like it was damaged. We found a large rock in the rose bushes beside the door, which we think the killer threw at the camera to disable it. Everything from six minutes prior to the call is blurry and distorted. It's clear that someone approached the house in that time but there's no way to identify who it is."

"Any luck on fingerprints or DNA?" Ryan had asked.

"No word yet on the latter, but the fingerprints came up empty," Watt said. "The only ones we definitively ID'd on the trophy were Sinclair's and a woman named Gail Musco, the emcee who handed it to her last night. And we checked—Musco left town for a holiday trip with her family this morning."

Soon after that disappointing conversation, they'd gotten a call from Officer Stoller, who had accompanied Marian Voytek back to the Vaughn Realty office.

"Ms. Voytek can't find any record of Clarissa Langley in their files," Stoller had told them. "She says that doesn't preclude them having ever met, perhaps at an open house or other event. But apparently Vaughn never formally worked with her."

Jessie knew that Ryan was thinking the same thing that she was: none of this was enough to take to Parker. The Ring camera neither helped nor hurt Vaughn. Nor did the lack of fingerprints on the trophy. That only confirmed that the killer was wearing gloves. And Jessie could hear Captain Parker in her head, making the very point that

Officer Stoller had. Not having Clarissa Langley as a client didn't prove that Vaughn didn't know her. It only proved that he hadn't created a file for her.

In desperation, Jessie had even gone back to Mitchell Vaughn to plead her case, this time notably without Ryan. She hoped that the man might provide something—anything—that could definitively allow them to eliminate him as a suspect. When she had walked into the interrogation room, Vaughn was sitting with his lawyer, a smallish man in his forties with a mustache and an aggressive comb-over, who handed her card that read: J. August Kinney.

"Mr. Kinney," she began, sitting down opposite both men, "I know your client has invoked his right to counsel, but I'm imploring both of you to reconsider his lack of cooperation."

"Why?" Kinney asked.

"Because, despite our initial interaction with Mr. Vaughn, I think there's a better than decent chance that he didn't commit these crimes," Jessie told him. "And if that's the case, then it means there's a killer out there while he's in here. But in order to convince my bosses of that, I have to have something to work with. If he can walk me through where he was over the last week, it could prove helpful to both him and us."

"How can my client know that you won't use what he says against him?" Kinney asked, sounding unconvinced.

"I can't promise anything," Jessie said, "but if he's not responsible for these murders, then nothing he says will incriminate him, and it might save other lives. As it is right now, the department is ready to recommend charges against your client. If you can give me a compelling reason to advise against that, it will prevent any future damage to his reputation *and* help us refocus on the real killer."

"Ms. Hunt," Kinney said, a smarmy smile on his face, "while I can assure you that Mr. Vaughn had nothing to do with these terrible crimes, and also convey that we wish you success in your investigation, solving this case is not his responsibility. Moreover, here's what I can promise you. If the LAPD holds a news conference, as I'm hearing it will, naming my client and recommending he be indicted for murder, this department will face a lawsuit unlike anything it's ever encountered before."

"There's no need for threats, Mr. Kinney," Jessie said.

"I beg to differ, Ms. Hunt," Kinney countered. "There is no physical evidence tying Mr. Vaughn to these killings. His arrest was based on hasty assumptions and circumstantial evidence that can be easily rebutted. Furthermore, he is a respected member of the city's business community, and you will be irrevocably besmirching his name, likely making it impossible for him to continue to make a living here. You would be taking this action despite direct warnings about the impact of making these allegations publicly. So let me be clear. Mr. Vaughn will not be cooperating with this department in any way. He expects to be released immediately. And if Chief Decker names him to the news media, rest assured that I will be at a microphone minutes later announcing a pending lawsuit against the department for a sum involving nine digits. Have I made myself clear?"

He had, which was why Jessie had now returned to the conference room more depressed than when she'd left it. Ryan hadn't even asked how the meeting had gone. It was all over her face.

"Anything from Jamil and Beth while I was gone?" she asked dejectedly.

"I haven't checked in with them lately," Ryan admitted. "I figured that if they had something, they would have called."

"Well, I'm at my wit's end," Jessie said, slumping in her chair. "The frustrating thing is that, even if Vaughn had given us alibis for the times of the murders, it wouldn't help much. Just like with Landon Powers and Danielle Robertson, he could have planted those canisters much earlier and set them to release at a time of his choosing."

Ryan shook his head in frustration, before raising his hand as if asking for permission to comment. Only he didn't wait.

"Maybe we check in with the families and staff of the victims again," he suggested. "It's possible that someone remembers Vaughn coming by recently. Unlike Powers and Robertson, who both went to these houses regularly, it would be odd for a relator to show up at their home if they didn't have business with him anymore."

"But that assumes that Vaughn might be our guy," Jessie reminded him, "and I don't think he is, so that line of inquiry would be following a dead-end lead."

Ryan was quiet for a moment, as if slightly afraid to say what was he was thinking.

"Go ahead," she told him. "I can tell you have something on your mind."

"Okay," he began carefully, "I get that you think Vaughn is wrong for this. And I'm inclined to agree with you. But nothing we've found exonerates him. And what we *have* found makes him the most likely culprit out of anyone we've encountered so far. Maybe it's time to stop trying to find holes in the case against him and start shoring it up. Is it possible that Parker isn't the only one being a little pig-headed here?"

Jessie sat with that for a moment, then stood up.

"Please don't get pissed," he begged.

"I'm not pissed," she told him, and it was true. "It's a fair point. I'll admit that I'm confident that I'm right about this, but maybe I'm holding on to that too tight. I think I just need to take a little break to clear my head, then come at this fresh. Do you mind if I step out, maybe call Hannah to check in on how Kat's doing?"

"I actually think that's a great idea," he said. "I'll be here when you get back."

She leaned over and gave him a kiss to reinforce that she wasn't upset with him. Then she left the conference room and walked down the long hallway that led to the back door of the West Los Angeles Station. She stepped outside and made her way to a concrete bench along the back wall of the building.

This place was the opposite of Central Station, which was old and dilapidated but had a charming central courtyard with grass, a tree, and multiple wooden benches. The scenery around here was much nicer, with dozens of palm trees swaying in the wind. But the outdoor break area was a fenced-in patch of asphalt with unforgiving benches. Since that was all she had, Jessie sat down, pulled out her phone, and let her finger hover over the screen.

She considered calling Kat directly but worried the conversation might take longer than she had right now. A surge of guilt hit her, as she realized she was avoiding her grieving friend in favor of a case. Trying to push the feeling out of her head, she called Hannah instead.

The call rang once and went straight to voicemail, a clear sign that her sister was either in the middle of something or just didn't want to be bothered. Hannah had even told her once, back in her junior year of high school, that she would sometimes let the phone ring once before declining it to let the caller know that they'd been rejected in favor of whatever she was doing at that moment. The thought was infuriating. Now, even her mental break was falling through.

Her thoughts drifted to her sister. Even though she had made so many strides, Hannah could still be stubborn and immature. Right now, she was helping out a woman in deep pain, but she could just as easily slip back into her high school mentality, where it didn't occur to her to think about anyone other than herself. She was technically an adult, and often acted like it. But sometimes she behaved like a little child.

As that realization hit her, Jessie felt an intense shudder that passed up through her body and into her brain, where an odd tingle lingered. She knew the sensation. She'd had it many times before. It almost always meant she was onto something, but that her mind hadn't yet wrapped itself around what. She couldn't put her finger on what her brain was trying to tell her, but she knew one thing: it wasn't about Hannah. It was about this case.

She got up and walked back inside. But this time she wasn't wandering listlessly. Now she was moving with a purpose.

CHAPTER TWENTY THREE

Hannah felt guilty.

Normally she would have accepted Jessie's call, but under the circumstances, she felt sure her sister would understand. This was more important.

She and Kat were sitting on the couch in her apartment, watching the video footage that Jenny the nurse had recorded of Hannah's hospital room conversation with Ash Pierce. Jenny had surreptitiously handed her a thumb drive with the recording as she left the floor's secure unit.

The video was grainy, and the audio was a little scratchy, but the entirety of their chat had been captured. When it ended, Hannah turned to Kat, who looked pale.

"What do you think?" she asked.

Kat shook her head.

"I think that I wasn't prepared for this," she conceded. "I went to that hospital room so many times when she was in a coma that I guess I got used to seeing her like that. But the sight of her now, sitting up and alert, is really disconcerting. Some part of me hoped that maybe she'd lost some mental acuity because of what happened. But she seems as sharp as before."

"I agree," Hannah said, noting that Kat hadn't addressed the larger issue, "but I mean, what did you think about her credibility? Do you think there's any chance that she's telling the truth, that she really did lose all memory of her time as a hitwoman for hire?"

Kat slumped back on the couch.

"I don't," she said, "but I'm not sure how much my opinion matters. This woman tricked me, as you well know. She gave a false identity and claimed to be an abused woman trying to hide from her husband, all as a ruse to get me to an isolated location so she could torture and kill me. If such a thing exists, you could probably show me a brain scan proving that she lost her memory, and I still wouldn't believe it. The real question is, did *you* believe her? You were in that room, talking to her face to face. You saw her micro-expressions and heard the variance in her voice in real time. Did you buy her story?"

Hannah slumped back on the couch as well. She knew this question would be coming, and she was no more confident in her answer now than before.

"I don't need to remind you that she snowed me too with the 'abused wife' persona, or that she wanted to torture and kill me too. Or that I had to hide in safe houses when she was hunting for me after she escaped from prison. I'm as biased as you are. So my initial impression is that she's full of it…"

"I think I hear a 'but' in there," Kat noted.

"But," Hannah said sheepishly. "I don't know if my conclusion is based on any actual evidence. I mean, there *were* a couple of moments that gave me pause."

"Like what," Kat wondered.

Hannah sighed as she tried to relive the memory. "One was when she mentioned getting stabbed in the neck when she was 'supposedly' trying to kill some young woman. I swear I thought I saw a flinch of recognition, like she knew I was the young woman she was referencing."

"And the other?" Kat asked.

"When I asked what job she would have that prepared her for murdering innocent people, she seemed slightly taken aback and coughed a little. I couldn't tell if she was stalling to come up with a convincing answer or if she was sincere in her confusion and stunned that I was so confrontational with her. But when I watch and listen to those parts of the exchanges on the video now, I'm not sure if it was just my imagination."

"The footage and the audio are just too compromised to determine anything like that," Kat pointed out. "What does your gut tell you?"

Hannah took a moment to really think about that question.

"My gut tells me that she's lying," she finally answered. "I think she knew who I was. And I still think that this is all an elaborate con game to either gain sympathy before a jury or get her security detail to lower their guard. But am I a hundred percent sure? No. She never made a false move or said a false word. She never gave any clear indication that she knew that I was testing her, or even that she knew who I was. She never misstepped. And if she *is* faking this, that's the scariest part."

"Why do you say that?" Kat asked.

"Because if she's operating at this level right now, only weeks out of waking from a coma and days after having major neck surgery, what will she be like when she's back at full strength?"

Kat ran her fingers through her dirty blonde hair, clearly troubled by the same issue.

"Maybe we could have Jessie talk to her," she suggested. "She's a professional criminal profiler."

"Maybe," Hannah replied, "but she's only had minimal interaction with Pierce. She hasn't seen her in action like we have. She hasn't seen her weave an entire false narrative about her life or coldly prepare to kill someone. I feel like we're better able to catch her in a mistake than Jessie is."

"What then?" Kat wondered, her tone irritable.

Suddenly, an idea occurred to Hannah.

"There's no question that Jessie is an amazing profiler," she said, "but I can think of someone else who has experience with that job, someone who used to work with the LAPD and the FBI, profiling killers, and then left that job to spend the last decade probing people's minds for more altruistic reasons."

"You're talking about Dr. Lemmon?" Kat assumed.

"I am," Hannah confirmed. "Think about it. She doesn't have any of the baggage that you or I, or even Jessie does. She's had decades of experience studying killers, as well as working with everyday people dealing with mental and emotional challenges, and she's an expert at telling the difference between the two. If she asked to interview Pierce, the LAPD would surely welcome her evaluation."

"But would Pierce?" Kat asked.

"That's the best part," Hannah said, warming to her own idea. "If she's legit, then she should welcome the opportunity to prove it to someone as respected as Dr. Janice Lemmon. And if she's lying, she has two options. She could refuse to talk with Lemmon for fear the doctor would uncover her deception, which would be a bad look. Or she'd view it as an opportunity to outmaneuver someone with unparalleled authority with law enforcement. If Lemmon gave her the 'all clear,' it would do wonders for her credibility. Whether she's telling the truth or not, Ash Pierce should want to leap at this chance."

As Hannah made the case, she saw something happen that had been incredibly rare in the last few days. She saw Kat break into a smile. If for no other reason than maintaining the hopeful grin on Kat Gentry's face, Hannah decided that this had to happen, and soon.

CHAPTER TWENTY FOUR

"You can't explain it to me?" Ryan asked, clearly frustrated as he sat across from Jessie at the conference room table.

She was equally exasperated. Not with him, but because she was unable to find the words to convey what was eating at her.

"I'm trying," she said, "but every time I think I've got a handle on the idea, it fades away, like I'm trying to grab a wisp of smoke."

"Okay," he said calmly, "tell me what you were thinking about when you got the tingly feeling."

"It was something about Hannah," she said, "and how, despite how far she's come, she can still be immature. That's when the bells went off in my head."

"What, like she reminded you of one of our suspects who was immature? Selfish maybe? That's certainly true of some of them, although we could say the same thing about some of victims too. Maybe that was it?"

"Maybe," Jessie said, unconvinced.

Ryan continued. It was clear to Jessie that he hoped that by throwing out suggestions, he might unlock whatever thought she couldn't access.

"Clarissa Langley, for one, seemed more interested in ensuring that her seven-year-old son gets into a good college than in letting him enjoy his holiday break," he noted. "And Naomi Hackett doesn't even live with her family during the week because she's so fixated on her tech startup."

Jessie was about to chastise Ryan for criticizing Hackett for the exact same professional "selfishness" that so many hard-charging men regularly displayed, when another thought burst into her brain. This wasn't about selfishness or immaturity. She'd been thinking about Hannah earlier because sometimes her little sister was still, at heart, just a kid. That was the idea that had been circling around in her head all this time: this was about the kids. She looked up at Ryan.

"Did we ever follow up on the GPS location data for our suspects other than Mitchell Vaughn?" she asked, "to determine when they were last at the victims' houses and make sure those dates and times matched what they told us?"

Ryan's face scrunched up in uncertainty.

"I think Jamil and Beth set those searches aside when our focus turned to Vaughn," he said.

"Let's see how far they got," she replied.

"Okay," Ryan said as he called the research office and put his phone on speaker. "Should we just start in order of how we found them: Powers, and then Robertson?"

"Actually," Jessie countered, "I think we should start with Danielle Robertson."

"Why?"

"I'm not sure yet," she admitted, "but I think all this has something to do with the victims' children."

"Hello?" Jamil said when the call connected.

"Hey guys," Jessie launched in, "Did you ever get the GPS location data from our earlier suspects' phones and vehicles?"

"We started," Jamil told her, "but we hadn't finished when we had to switch our attention to Vaughn. But our preliminary data validated everything from their statements."

"Even for Danielle Robertson?" Jessie pressed.

"Like I said, we hadn't finished, but what we've pulled to date backs up her claims."

Jessie realized she'd been holding her breath in anticipation of something that wasn't forthcoming and exhaled in frustration.

"Why are you so interested in Danielle Robertson?" Ryan asked, "Do you really think, based on our interview with her, that she would put the kids she worked with at risk by exposing them to canisters full of poison?"

"No, I don't," Jessie conceded, slightly embarrassed, before the brain tingle returned, more potent than ever before. She continued excitedly, "I don't believe that! And that's why we need to do a deeper dive on her."

"What are you thinking?" Ryan asked, clearly sensing that she thought she was on to something big.

"Think about it," she said, having trouble getting her words out as fast as they entered her head. "The canisters in each of these women's homes released the poison when their children weren't around. Tabitha Reynolds's daughter, Susannah, was on a camping trip with her ex-husband. Remember, the coroner told us that we caught a lucky break because no one else was in her loft at the time the poison was released. Otherwise, we could have had multiple victims. But what if that wasn't luck at all?"

Ryan looked like he wanted to respond, but Jessie was on a roll now and not about to stop.

"And think about all the other victims," she continued. "Clarissa Langley's son, Lansing, was at a Clippers game with his father. And Naomi Hackett's daughter, Olivia, was at the family's Pacific Palisades home when Hackett was murdered at her Playa Vista apartment. They were all safely out of danger at the time the poison was released. And other than their parents, who would know those kinds of details about these kids' schedules? How about their private tutor, who could easily ask them about their upcoming plans without drawing suspicion."

Ryan was quiet and there was silence on the other end of the phone line, suggesting that Jamil and Beth were also pondering her theory.

"That's interesting," Ryan finally said, "But aren't you forgetting something? Danielle Robertson never taught Olivia Hackett at the Playa Vista apartment, so how would she have gotten in there?"

Jessie had an answer for that one.

"First of all, that conclusion is based on what Robertson told us. We don't know if it's true. And even if it is, that doesn't mean she was being honest about never visiting the apartment. Maybe she casually 'stopped by' one day. It wouldn't be crazy. She lives in Westchester. That's only minutes from Hackett's apartment. And Playa Vista is all mixed use. There are condos and apartments right next to ice cream parlors and sushi bars. How hard would it be to manufacture an unexpected run-in? If that happened, I could easily see Hackett inviting Robertson up to her place for a minute. Or maybe Danielle asked to use her bathroom? In either case, who would be able to tell us about it? Naomi Hackett is dead. The only person who would ever know is Robertson. That's why we need to check her GPS location data for recent stops anywhere near Hackett's apartment."

"Checking now," Jamil said. Jessie could hear his fingers flying across his keyboard.

"I hate to constantly be negative," Ryan said, "But that's not the only speed bump here. Let's not forget that Avery Sinclair didn't even employ Danielle Robertson as a tutor. We have no evidence that they knew each other at all."

Jessie sat with that for a moment, but only that long.

"That's true," she agreed, "but she did have kids, right?"

"Yes, two," Beth interjected. "A four-year-old daughter named Riley and an eight-year-old son named Rhett."

"Okay," Jessie continued, "The girl is a little young, but the boy is right in Robertson's tutoring age window. And Sinclair lived in the Palisades, where we know Robertson had at least one other client, Naomi Hackett."

"Actually," Beth volunteered, "From her client roster, it looks like five of the kids she worked with lived in that area."

Jessie gave Ryan a satisfied grin.

"So then how surprising would it be for Avery Sinclair to have heard about Danielle Robertson from other parents, and maybe even talked to her at some point about hiring her?"

"Bad news," Beth said. "We already cross-checked every victim's phone logs for the last three months with every suspect, and there's not one call between Avery Sinclair or her husband and Danielle Robertson."

Jessie's grin faded. She was stumped. Everything in her told her she was headed down the right road, but she kept meeting roadblocks.

"Beth," Ryan said, a flicker of light in his eyes. "Can you check the call logs of any of Robertson's Palisades-area clients, say for the last month, and see if any of them had calls with Avery Sinclair?"

"Give me a minute," Beth said.

Jessie smiled at Ryan. "Am I turning you into a believer?" she asked.

"Don't get ahead of yourself, Hunt," he replied. "This could be nothing."

Moments later, Beth contradicted him.

"It's not nothing," she said eagerly.

"What do you mean?" Jessie asked.

"One of Danielle Robertson's clients is a woman named Shane Willoughby, whose son is eight, just like Avery Sinclair's. And Willoughby clearly knew Sinclair."

"Why do you say that?" Ryan asked.

"Because I count nine calls between them this month alone, some as long as forty-five minutes. I'm guessing that either Sinclair was Willoughby's real estate agent or the two of them were friends."

Jessie looked over at Ryan, doing her best to hide the mix of expectation and anticipation she felt. But she failed miserably, as another hopeful smile peeked out.

Ryan shook his head, trying not to give in to her enthusiasm. Still, when he spoke, she could tell he was starting to buy in.

"Do you want to call Willoughby or should I?"

CHAPTER TWENTY FIVE

Jessie decided to make the phone call.

She figured, and Ryan agreed, that it would raise fewer alarm bells if she initiated contact with Shane Willoughby. She also thought that if they could get their information without bringing up Sinclair's death, it would simplify things, so she made no mention of it.

"We're looking into issues related to inappropriate behavior by a local male tutor and wanted your input," she explained after introducing herself.

"Oh, that's horrible," Willoughby exclaimed. "Who are you investigating?"

"I'm afraid that I'm not at liberty to reveal that," Jessie told her.

"I certainly understand but I'm not sure how much help I can offer," Willoughby said. "Our tutor is female."

"Who's that?" Jessie wondered innocently.

"Her name is Danielle Robertson," Willoughby replied, "and she's wonderful."

"In that case, maybe you could give us the names of her other clients so we can exclude them from future calls. I don't want to upset parents unnecessarily."

"Sure," she said, listing off a series of names, all of which Jessie was already familiar with.

"That's incredibly helpful," she said, before adding nonchalantly. "What about Avery and Willem Sinclair? I have them on my call list as well."

"Oh, you can skip them too," Willoughby assured her. "They don't have a tutor at all, although they might be considering hiring Danielle."

"What makes you say that?" Jessie asked, forcing down the rising excitement in her throat.

"Just that Avery was at our place a few weeks ago for a girls' night and Danielle—she likes the kids to call her Junior, by the way—was working with my son, Braden. He and Avery's boy, Rhett, are the same age and she asked if Danielle was helpful. I started singing her praises, so they talked briefly, and Avery took her number."

"So Avery was going to hire her for sure?"

"I wouldn't go that far," Willoughby said. "Avery seemed convinced, but I'm not sure Danielle was."

"Why not?" Jessie asked.

"Because Avery was, for lack of a better word, kind of bitchy to her. Avery has a lot of good qualities, but she can be sharp-elbowed with her barbs, and she was tossing them off fast and furious that day. Danielle knows how to deal with entitled people. Hell, I'm entitled. But Avery is *a lot*, and the poor girl looked a little put off. I'm not sure she wanted to deal with someone so biting on a regular basis."

"Thanks very much, Mrs. Willoughby," Jessie said. She felt like she had more than enough.

"Of course," the woman replied. "Let me know if you need anything else. I just want our children to be safe."

Jessie had barely hung up with Willoughby before she was suggesting a theory to Ryan and the researchers, who had been on speaker the whole time.

"I think I can explain why Sinclair was killed with that trophy instead of the poison," she said.

"Please," Ryan asked. He clearly knew better than to get in the way when she was on a roll.

"If Sinclair wasn't a client yet, there was no easy way to plant a poison canister in her house," Jessie said. "That means she would either have had to talk her way in, maybe at a scheduled meeting, or perhaps an impromptu one. Either way, I think that when she tried to plant the canister in Avery Sinclair's bedroom, Sinclair found her. A struggle ensued, with Sinclair dead from blunt force trauma and Robertson rushing out because the poison canister went off accidentally."

"Ms. Hunt?" Jamil said cautiously.

"You're not going to shoot down my theory, are you, Jamil?"

"No," he assured her. "I have some new information, but I didn't want to interrupt you."

"Interrupt away," she told him.

"I got more robust GPS data for Danielle Robertson's movements in recent months," he said, "and I do find multiple instances of both her vehicle and phone in the Playa Vista area in the last couple of weeks. Neither of them are ever within more than a couple of hundred yards of Naomi Hackett's apartment but she was definitely nearby. The last time she was there was on Saturday."

Jessie viewed the information as a net positive.

"As far as I'm concerned, none of that disproves my theory," she insisted. "Robertson could have just left her phone in her car while she went to Hackett's apartment."

"That's certainly possible," Ryan agreed, "and you've offered a more than credible theory. Unfortunately, everything about it is just as circumstantial as the case we have against Vaughn, maybe more so."

"What do you mean?" Jessie wanted to know.

"Well, for one thing, Danielle Robertson isn't exactly an imposing figure," he said. "Avery Sinclair was taller than her. I could more easily see Vaughn getting the upper hand on her in a struggle. And Robertson doesn't seem like any more of a science expert than Vaughn. We can certainly talk to her again, but unless we have something more bulletproof, I don't see Parker recommending that Chief Decker postpone his news conference."

Jessie knew that Ryan wasn't intentionally trying to undercut her. He was just doing his job, poking the same holes in the case that Parker would. But it was still frustrating. She tried to focus on the merits of his arguments and not take it personally. As she pondered what he'd said, one point he'd made struck her as unconvincing.

"Are we sure that Robertson isn't more knowledgeable about science than we're giving her credit for? She is an aspiring teacher after all, and just because she said that she didn't understand upper level stuff doesn't make it true."

"What did she say she majored in again?" Ryan tried to recall. "Was it Child Development?"

"That *was* her major," Beth informed them, the tone of her voice suggesting she had come across something interesting. "But reviewing her academic records, it looks like she only switched to that after her freshman year."

"What was it before that?" Jessie asked excitedly.

Beth paused for a long beat before answering.

"Biochemistry."

Jessie felt a sudden desire to punch her fist in the air. But before she even got the chance, she heard a familiar voice on the other end of the line.

"Excuse me," Captain Parker said. She had apparently walked into the research department back at Central Station. "I know you all are in the thick of it right now, but I need to take a moment of your time."

The odd formality in Parker's voice sent a shiver through Jessie. Something was terribly wrong.

“Is Dr. Lemmon okay?” she demanded immediately.

“As far as I know, she’s fine, Ms. Hunt,” Parker told her. "This is about something else. Hank Costabile is missing."

The shiver that Jessie had felt moments earlier turned into a full-body quake.

CHAPTER TWENTY SIX

Jessie wasn't sure she had heard the words properly.

Her brain had been so focused on the case that recalibrating it to think about Costabile took a moment. But Ryan didn't have that problem.

"What the hell happened?" he demanded.

"Apparently the officers tailing him lost him at a Hollywood area Metro station," Parker said.

"How long ago did this happen?" Jessie asked, managing to regroup slightly. She looked at the time. It was 3:49.

"About twenty minutes ago," Parker said. "We've got officers checking every Metro stop for ten miles in either direction. We think we've got a lead on his plans though."

"What are they?" Ryan pressed.

"Officer Daniel Carrera, who was one of Costabile's assigned tails for the day, spoke to a homeless man who got in his way while he was searching for Costabile. He found it suspicious, and after some basic questioning, the man admitted that Costabile paid him to provide a distraction. The man also said that Costabile mentioned something about getting down to San Diego and crossing the border into Tijuana."

"Why would he reveal that?' Ryan asked skeptically. "It sounds like something he'd say to throw us off his scent while he was staying here or going somewhere else."

"You may be right," Parker conceded. "However, we did find a record of him purchasing a ticket on the Pacific Surfliner train, which left Union Station for San Diego a few minutes ago. We have someone headed to catch it to see if he's actually on it. But whether we find him or not, I don't know that there's much we can do about it."

"Why not?" Beth asked.

Jessie had the answer to that question, though she didn't like it.

"Because officially, he hasn't done anything wrong," she said. "Even though he was released from prison on a technicality, he's a free man. He can go wherever he wants. Chief Decker only assigned those officers to watch him because he was worried that Costabile might pursue a vendetta against me. And maybe he intends to. But it's just as possible that he got sick of having a couple of cops following him around wherever he went and decided to bust loose of them for a few hours. He could be at a friend's house or a strip club blowing off steam. Even if they find him, and I'm not sure they will, what can they do? Arrest him for slipping their tail?"

"All of that is true," Parker acknowledged, "but just the same, Chief Decker has asked me to ensure that precautions are taken in case he didn't really leave town. Two officers are being sent to your home in case Costabile tries to sneak in. We'd also like to post two more to watch your sister in case he goes after her. My understanding is that she's staying at Kat Gentry's place to help her out during her time of grieving."

"That's correct," Jessie said, not asking how Parker knew that detail.

"That will make it easier," the captain said, "better to have them in the same place."

"I appreciate that," Jessie told her.

"Not a problem," Parker said. "I'd also like you to keep us apprised of your location as you pursue this case. Just let the dispatch sergeant know about any stops you make, and he'll make sure that a squad car is in the immediate vicinity. That is, unless you prefer we just have a car follow you wherever you go tonight."

Jessie looked at Ryan, who shrugged.

"I don't have a problem with it," he said.

He might not, but Jessie did.

"I don't think that's necessary," she said. "Costabile doesn't have any clue where we'll be, and I don't want to scare off any witnesses or suspects we talk to by having a squad car right behind us the whole time. Besides, the man isn't an idiot. Even if he does have it in for me, he know we'll be on high alert until he's found. He's not going to try anything stupid after just getting out of prison. So no on the tail thanks, Captain. But having a squad car in the area is probably a good idea."

"I'll arrange it with the dispatch sergeant," Parker said. "Just call when you get moving. By the way, *do* you have any new suspects?"

"That's what we're trying to determine right now," Jessie told her, not wanting to get into a back-and-forth about Robertson until she was confident enough to plead her case.

"Alright, then I'll leave you to it," Parker said.

After several seconds of silence, Beth spoke.

"She's gone now."

"Can you shut the door, Beth?" they heard Jamil say quietly.

Jessie and Ryan exchanges a curious glance, waiting to see why the researcher was suddenly being so cautious.

Once they heard the door close, Jessie asked.

"Why so secretive, Jamil?"

"Because while you were all talking, I found something else," he said, "but I didn't exactly come by it legitimately, so I didn't want the captain to know."

"Color me intrigued," Jessie said. "What is it?"

Jamil sighed.

"I don't feel great about this, but I think it was worth the risk," he said. "I was going through Danielle Robertson's personal information, and I found a reference to her having a juvenile record. As with all juvenile files, it's sealed and inaccessible without a court order. But I hacked the system anyway."

Everyone was quiet for a moment, stunned that a straight arrow like Jamil Winslow would do such a thing.

"We can deal with the moral issues associated with that decision later," Ryan eventually said with mild disapproval. "But since it's already done, what did you find?"

"Apparently when she was in middle school, Robertson was the victim of vicious bullying," Jamil said. "It started out with teasing and name-calling. Other girls would refer to her as "Junior" and "Chip" as in 'chip off the old block' because her last name was Robertson, as in "Robert's son." Really dumb stuff. But it eventually escalated to the point where some girls would text her, telling her that she should kill herself."

"Oh my god," Jessie muttered.

Jamil continued, clearly attempting to push through because the material was so unpleasant.

"This group of girls apparently cornered her in a classroom after school one day and relentlessly berated her, telling her different ways that she should end things. When one of them shoved her against the teacher's desk, Robertson grabbed a stapler and began beating that girl about the head with it. The other girls called a teacher for help. By the time Robertson was pulled off the first girl, she was unconscious. She ended up losing an eye."

No one could think of anything to say, so Jamil pressed on.

"She was going to be sent to a juvenile detention facility, but when the enormity of the bullying she faced was uncovered, her lawyer managed to get her placed in a diversion program at a psychiatric facility. When she was released a year later, her family moved to a different town for high school. There were no subsequent issues listed in her record. She graduated with honors, got into a great school and graduated in four years. You know the rest."

"So are we thinking that the horrors she suffered in middle school a dozen years ago made her some kind of ticking time bomb that exploded this week?" Beth asked.

"It could be more complicated than that," Jessie said. "We don't know what kind of indignities she suffered in that psychiatric facility. She may come out seeming recovered, but it's possible that she just shoved down whatever was churning inside her."

She looked at Ryan, whose expression suggested he was less skeptical than before. But she could tell he still wanted more. She gave it to him.

"Plus, we all heard what Shane Willoughby said. It seems like Avery Sinclair was the adult version of the mean girls that Danielle knew as a teenager. I don't know about Tabitha Reynolds or Naomi Hackett, but Clarissa Langley didn't sound like a barrel of laughs. Maybe the accumulation of nastiness from these women eventually made her snap."

"Maybe," Ryan conceded, "but that's still not as direct a motive as Mitchell Vaughn losing a realtor award to Avery Sinclair last night and her ending up pummeled to death with that very award today. I realize we don't have motives yet for him with the other women, but that doesn't mean they don't exist."

Jessie couldn't disagree, even if she felt increasingly confident that Robertson was their killer. She wracked her brain for something so substantial that even Ryan couldn't dismiss it. And then it hit her. In all her haste to make the pieces fit, she'd passed over the one tidbit that Robertson had provided for them.

"Hold on, Jamil," she said, "didn't you say that Robertson's school bullies called her 'Junior?'"

"Yes, that and Chip."

Jessie stared hard at Ryan.

"Shane Willoughby told us that Danielle preferred the kids call her Junior. Why do that when the name is fraught with so much pain?"

"Maybe that was her way of taking ownership of the word so that it lost its power over her," he offered.

"Or maybe she never really got over it," Jessie countered, "and having children call her that was a way of continuing to beat herself up all these years later."

Ryan gave a relenting shrug.

"It's not the craziest theory I've heard,"

"Thanks for the support," she replied with a playful smirk, before focusing her attention on the researchers on speakerphone.

"Hey guys, can you do a search of Danielle Robertson's GPS location status to determine when—?"

"She was last at the other victims' homes?" Jamil interrupted. "Already been working on it for the last minute."

Jessie was always impressed by the brilliant young man. She waited quietly to hear what he'd discovered.

"It looks like she was at all their homes in the last ten days," he told them all.

"She could have planted the canisters on those visits," Jessie posited.

"That makes sense," Beth ventured. "Maybe she was worried that if she left them any earlier than that, the canisters might be discovered."

"Possible," Ryan said, getting in on it now too, "or maybe the poison in the canisters has some kind of expiration date after which it's not effective."

Jessie, who thought both those suspicions were credible, had already moved on. The thought of canisters sitting in people's homes, just waiting for the push of a button, filled her with anxiety. They had to find out who the next victim was going to be.

"We need to compile a list of any other client that she visited in the last ten days," she announced. "We should include mothers who were as hardcore as the victims were about their kids being tutored during winter break."

"Working on it now," Jamil replied.

"Should we focus on divorced women?" Ryan wondered. "Robertson seems to prioritize keeping other family members safe when the canisters go off. If they're at their dads' places, the potential victim might be alone."

"It's a parameter worth including," Jessie agreed, "but we shouldn't limit it to that. Three of our four victims were married. I'm betting the reasons these women were chosen had more to do with subjective criteria in Robertson's head than anything we can easily pin down."

"I find three other clients that Robertson visited in the last ten days," Jamil announced. "Grace Barber lives in Venice. Sienna Ford lives in Marina del Rey. So does Ashley Bailey. And for the record, she is divorced."

"Any chance you can see if Robertson's GPS shows her near any of their homes?" Ryan asked.

"Actually," Beth said, "it's had her at her Westchester apartment ever since she gave us authorization to access her data. Is it weird that neither her car nor her phone have moved at all since 11 a.m.?"

"She could just be binging a TV show," Jessie admitted, "or she could have left them at her place while she went out in a cab that she paid cash for, knowing she was being tracked."

"Why would she leave that stuff at home unless she was going somewhere she didn't want us to know about?" Ryan asked.

"An excellent question," Jessie said. "One, I think we should ask her. But let's do it on the way to the car."

"Where are we going?" he asked.

"All three of the clients Jamil listed live south of the station," Jessie said. "Let's head in that direction, working our way from one home to the next. While we call Robertson, Beth and Jamil can reach out to these women to find out where they are right now. It's the Friday afternoon of a long holiday weekend. There's no guarantee they're all at home. We need to know where they are and if they're safe."

She stood up and grabbed her bag. Ryan got up too.

"We'll call you back as soon as we get status updates on the clients," Beth told them before hanging up.

As Jessie and Ryan headed along the hallway of the West Los Angeles police station toward the parking lot, she called Danielle Robertson's cell phone. It went straight to voicemail. She redialed. The same thing happened. She looked over at Ryan as the pushed through the station's outer door.

"No answer," she told him.

His face scrunched up into a grimace as he replied.

"That is definitely not good."

CHAPTER TWENTY SEVEN

As Sienna Ford parked her car in the garage of her oceanfront Marina del Rey home, she pulled out her phone.

She had just dropped off Candace. And with that final, major responsibility of the day complete, she did one last check for missed voicemails and texts. Finding none, she did something she'd been looking forward to all day: she put her phone on silent.

With her husband, Paul, currently crossing the Atlantic Ocean for an emergency investor meeting in Brussels that would keep him away over Christmas, she knew he wouldn't be calling tonight. In fact, since it was 4 p.m. here, it was already the middle of the night on his plane. He might even be asleep.

And now that Candace was 10, she'd developed a real independent streak. When she went to a friend's house for a sleepover, as she was doing tonight, she often refused to even answer her phone for a final "good night" and "I love you" call. Sienna would probably have to reach out to Rianne, the mother of Candace's friend, Lissa, and make her bring her own phone to Candace for the obligatory call. But that wasn't for a while.

Sienna estimated that she had a good five hours before she had to worry about such things. Which meant she had five hours of uninterrupted alone time. No work calls about the gallery opening next month. No family to feed. No friends coming over. Just Sienna time.

She had a lot of important action items on the agenda. First, she'd start with a bubble bath, before eventually moving on to some white wine, girl dinner, and at least three episodes of *Top Chef*. It was going to be a wild night.

She walked into the kitchen and threw her keys in the basket on the counter before pulling off her high heels and making her way directly to the bedroom. Her calves were killing her, and she intended to soak them for quite some time.

"Alexa, play Sade," she called out to the voice assistant as she made her way down the hallway to the bedroom.

"No Ordinary Love" came on as she entered the bedroom and began to undress, laying her clothes on the bed. Clad only in her bra and underwear, she made her way into the bathroom, intent on finding her favorite bathrobe. As she passed in front of the vanity mirror, she stopped and stared at herself.

At 34, she thought she was doing a decent job of fighting the battle against time. She'd had Candace when she was just 24 and still in graduate school, getting her master's in art history. Unlike some of her friends who had kids after thirty, she'd managed to bounce back physically pretty quickly. It helped that Paul was making $300K by the time Candace was born, affording Sienna the freedom to work with a personal trainer *and* a personal chef.

Still, so far at least, she'd managed to stay firm without artificial assistance. Deciding that she'd admired herself long enough, Sienna tied her jet-black hair in a bun. She wanted a nice bath, but without getting bubbles in her hair.

She found the lavender robe on the back hook of her walk-in closet door and put it on. It occurred to her that she was being unnecessarily modest, considering that she was alone in the house. Years of worrying about a little girl barging in on her had made her needlessly cautious.

She turned on the water in the bath, got it to the preferred temperature, then added the bubble bath soap. The noise from the water was loud, so she instructed Alexa to increase the volume on Sade. While she waited for the tub to fill, she returned to the bedroom to take off her other clothes.

She moved fast as she wanted to get in the tub soon. For one thing, she deserved it. And for another, she suddenly felt an odd chill in the air.

CHAPTER TWENTY EIGHT

Junior watched closely from the safety of the closet, making sure not to breathe too loud.

At first, she was concerned that any minor joint crack would reveal her location in Paul Ford's walk-in closet. But that fear quickly subsided when Sienna Ford started piping music into the bathroom.

There was a moment of anxiety when Sienna stared at her bathroom vanity counter. Junior was sure that the woman had noticed the metal canister that had been placed just behind her husband's Costco mega-sized bottle of mouthwash. But it quickly became clear that Sienna was intently studying her own body, not the items in front of her.

There was a second fearful moment when Sienna approached the closet. As she drew closer, Junior gripped the three-iron golf club that she'd found in the back of the closet. But Sienna veered left, going to her own closet and putting on a bathrobe over her bra and panties. Junior sighed quietly.

She became even more confident when Sienna turned on the water in the bathtub and jacked up the music. Now, no amount of joint cracking or heavy breathing would betray her position. In fact, she could probably walk right out and bash Sienna in the head without the woman ever realizing she was there.

And Sienna Ford would deserve it, just like the others did. Maybe she wasn't as overtly objectionable as some of them were, but her relentless pressure on her ten-year-old daughter was just as insidious.

She might think that having the girl attend "art workshops" twice during the week and on weekends, not to mention thrice-weekly ballet lessons, wasn't as bad as making her do math worksheets every night. But because of all the extra-curriculars, Candace missed tons of school and had fallen behind, necessitating the 8 p.m. tutoring sessions that usually lasted at least an hour. The poor thing rarely got to sleep before ten, far too late for a child her age. And it was having an impact.

Candace was a nasty piece of work, constantly mocking the size and grace of other girls in both ballet and school. Sienna either didn't seem to know or care that her constant emphasis on her own body image had been subtly inculcated in her daughter, who refused to have snacks more caloric than jicama or celery while studying.

But like the children of the other women that Junior had excised, there was still hope for Candace. She was young enough that a drastic change in her life could make a difference. That was the twin goal of Junior's efforts.

First, by cutting out the malignant mothers, who were slowly poisoning their children's capacity for empathy and kindness, Junior offered the kids a path to redemption. Without the offending parent, they were far less likely to become vicious teens, capable of destroying another child's life with relentless bullying. Nor would they grow into people like their mothers, cruel and hateful, passing on their vitriol to another generation.

Secondly, by ripping them away from the controlling bosoms of their mothers, these children would face a shocking, painful loss early in their lives. The hope was that the heartache they felt would heighten their ability to identify and ease that pain in others. And Junior had made a personal commitment to be there to help these kids through that difficult journey.

But for Candace Ford, the journey to decency could only begin with the sacrifice of her mother, just as it had for Lansing Langley, Samantha Reynolds, Olivia Hackett, and Rhett Sinclair. These children could still be saved, but only at a price.

As Junior watched Sienna Ford retreat to her bedroom, she couldn't help but marvel once again at the deliciously poetic nature of these women's demise. They had poisoned their children's minds, and now they were quite literally being poisoned. The poetry was her brainchild, though the method wasn't.

Junior still remembered when she'd first thought of the idea of using botulinum toxin as a poison. It was during her third month at the Ridgewood Psychiatric Care Facility for Young People. One of her fellow residents, a brilliant young man named Kenny Littrell, had mentioned a fantasy about using it in group discussion.

The therapist leading the group wasn't excited about his comments, but Junior—or Danielle, as she let others there call her—was intrigued. She'd made Kenny—who was in the facility for repeatedly setting small fires at home and school—tell her everything he knew about the concept.

Junior was sad when he was released back into the wilds of society a couple of months later, apparently cured of his pyromania, but she never forgot what she'd learned from him. And when she went to college, she was still interested enough in the science behind the concept to make biochemistry her major.

Eventually, her fury over what was done to her in school faded and she decided move on, focusing her energy on educating kids who deserved better than she got. And that was great for a while. Her enthusiasm for becoming a teacher was a salve against the nightmares that invaded her sleep. Her excitement at helping an entire generation of kids meet their untapped potential temporarily muted the echoes of voices in her head, the ones telling her that she wasn't good enough, pretty enough, smart enough—that her family would be happier if she was dead.

That was why she took the job as a tutor for these wealthy families—because the money would expedite her ability to get credentialed, pursue her master's degree, and help kids in need. But she hadn't been prepared for what she faced.

These weren't just kids who needed help with subtraction or understanding prepositions. They were the scions of uber-rich, super-accomplished parents who expected their children— some barely in kindergarten—to attend Ivy League schools or the equivalent. They pushed these kids, demanding that Junior drill them ceaselessly, forcing them to give up playdates and sleepovers and any free time at all in order to maximize their potential for an impressive future.

Junior had been struggling with her role in this process for a while now. The guilt was exacerbated when she accepted payment to tutor some of these kids during what should have been their holiday breaks. But what finally made her crack was when seven-year-old Lansing Langley had joked that a kid in his class was such a "retard" that he'd be lucky to get into a trade school. A seven-year-old boy said that! Worse, Clarissa Langley had laughed at the comment, before realizing her error and correcting him.

"Don't use that word," she scolded. "If a teacher hears it, you could get suspended. Then you'll be the retard in trade school."

Junior remembered thinking that the woman must be making some kind of sick joke. But she'd meant it. Later that same night, Junior had gone to the home of Shane Willoughby to tutor her eight-year-old son, Braden. While they worked on his multiplication tables, she could hear Shane and a friend talking in the other room over wine. The friend, who she later learned was named Avery Sinclair, was talking about a girl in her son's class, and how the girl forgot her line in the winter play.

"If I was that girl," she said acidly, "I would have gone home and slit my wrists that very night. Frankly, if I thought I could get away with it, I would have whispered that very advice to her after the show. I mean, why draw out the suffering that she's in for later in life, right? Just end it and save her parents the next ten years of public mortification."

Something inside Junior shifted that night. She realized that helping these kids wasn't enough. She could never teach them to change when their mothers were there, constantly pushing back, seeding them with evil intent. For it to be a fair fight, for these kids to have any kind of chance at a future, the offending element had to be removed. Once she came to that realization, everything else fell into place.

It was quite simple after that. She went home that evening and dived in, doing all kinds of research on how to most effectively concentrate gaseous botulinum toxin for maximum, rapid impact. It was amazing what one could do with a science background and access to the dark web. She studied how to use a timer-based, motion-activated canister to safely contain and then release the gas. Then she tested it.

Amazingly, with her background and a willingness to forego sleep, she had a working prototype in just weeks. When Lansing Langley mentioned at his tutoring session last week that he and his dad would be going to a Clippers game on Wednesday, Junior knew it was time. Clarissa would be home alone all afternoon and evening.

So at Lansing's final tutoring session of the year on Monday, Junior had brought the canister. It hadn't been hard to slip away and place it in Clarissa's bedroom. Then, at the appropriate time, she had activated it. The experiment was a smashing success, at least according to the news. It worked again with Tabitha Reynolds. And then with Naomi Hackett.

Naomi had been a masterstroke, as well as the reason that Junior knew she wouldn't be caught. Until late last week, she'd never even been to Naomi's Playa Vista apartment. But she had a key, given to her by Naomi on the off chance that Olivia ever spent the night there and needed a tutoring session. It had never happened because Naomi would never deign to see her child during the week, much less bring her to her private getaway.

So Junior had gone to Playa Vista on a Saturday, when the community hosted a farmers' market, which Naomi had told her she frequented religiously. Junior left her phone in her car so that it wouldn't show her exact location. Then she'd waited out of sight, near

Naomi's apartment, until she left for the market. The rest was simple. Junior unlocked the front door, planted the canister, and left the apartment in less than thirty seconds.

Avery Sinclair had been harder. Junior didn't yet have access to her home. But because the woman's words about that poor girl who'd forgotten her line in the play resonated so deeply in her memory, she decided that she couldn't wait.

That was why she had showed up at Sinclair's house today, even though the woman hadn't formally agreed to hire her as a tutor. And that was why she had made the reckless decision to sneak upstairs and hide the canister on Sinclair's bookshelf.

Of course, that plan had turned to crap. But not without a stunning silver lining. When Junior had been forced to use that trophy to protect herself from Sinclair's aggressive advance, she made an unexpected discovery.

While the poison gas canisters may have delivered poetic retribution, a sharp chunk of marble offered more immediate, visceral satisfaction. Until this afternoon, she had never gotten to personally see the impact of her efforts. She had to imagine them and check news reports for verification that they'd worked.

But watching Avery Sinclair's head cave in under the weight of her multiple blows left no doubt. And perhaps more importantly, it felt amazing. The sight of that vile bitch's blood pouring out of her skull gave her a thrill she'd never experienced before in her life. The feeling of being up close and personal as someone else's life just...ended—of being the reason for it—was a rush she hadn't known was possible. And she wanted it again.

That was why, even though she'd taken a cab here, she snuck into the Ford house through the backyard doggy door (the family dog had died six months ago, but the door hadn't gone anywhere) and set up the canister on the counter in Sienna Ford's bathroom, she felt like something was missing. And it was why, when she saw Paul Ford's golf club in the corner of his closet, she knew that when it came down to it, she'd be using that as her weapon of choice.

She snapped out of her vengeful trance when Sienna returned to the bathroom. The tub was full, and the song had changed. "The Sweetest Taboo" was now playing. Junior smiled to herself. She suspected that her interpretation of what taboo was sweetest might differ from Sade's.

Now all she had to do was decide: did she want to kill Sienna now, as she prepared to get into the tub, mistakenly thinking that she was about to have a relaxing afternoon? Or should she wait until Sienna was getting out, wet and vulnerable.

Either way, the woman would pay. And Junior would save another child's future.

CHAPTER TWENTY NINE

"We're a minute out," Ryan said.

"This has got to be the one," Jessie told him. "You know that, right?"

She realized that she was telling a seasoned detective something that was obvious to him, but her anxiety was getting the better of her.

"I know," he said as he yanked the steering wheel hard right, turning onto Sienna Ford's street. He turned off the siren so as not to announce their impending arrival.

Of course, he knew they were at the right place, just as she did. It hadn't taken long for them to determine that Ford had to be the next intended victim. While Jessie was repeatedly calling Danielle Robertson's cell phone and getting no reply and Ryan was informing Captain Parker that Chief Decker should definitely postpone his news conference, Jamil and Beth had called the three women that they all thought were the most likely next victims.

Jamil had reached Grace Barber, who lived in Venice. She was home with her family, which included her husband and two children. Even though it seemed unlikely that Danielle would release the poisoned canister if the kids were at home, Jamil told Grace the basic situation and instructed her to immediately take the whole family into their backyard, outside the confines of an enclosed room, and wait there until a squad car arrived.

Beth got ahold of Ashley Bailey, the divorcee from Marina del Rey. But she wasn't home. In fact, she was clear across the country, on a holiday trip to New York with her kids. They were just wrapping up dinner before going to see a Broadway show.

That only left the other Marina del Rey resident, Sienna Ford, to contact. Neither Jamil nor Beth could reach her on her phone. Attempts to call her husband were equally unsuccessful. That combination of factors was enough to have Ryan put both the siren and cherry light on his car and speed down the 405 freeway, and then the 90 freeway before it dead-ended not far from Ford's address.

By the time he pulled onto Outrigger Street as he shut off the siren, it was 4:28. They had made incredible time, all things considered. But as she jumped out of the passenger seat, Jessie feared it wouldn't be nearly fast enough. Sienna Ford could already be dead. And the house they were approaching might currently be filled with poisonous gas that they couldn't identify until it was too late.

It was only as she rushed across the front yard toward the home that she realized they hadn't thought to bring gas masks. She stopped on the porch of the house and turned to remind Ryan of their mistake. He stood right behind her with his weapon drawn.

"Should we try the door, or should I just toss one of these patio chairs through the front window?" he asked as he caught his breath.

Jessie was just about to warn him about the risk of poisonous air inside when the front door shot open and a completely naked woman sprinted out of it, leapt off the porch, and dashed into the front yard. Jessie recognized her immediately, despite the fact that she was dripping wet with what looked like bubbles all over her.

"She's trying to kill me!" the woman screamed.

"Sienna!" Jessie yelled at her, trying to calm her down.

The woman turned around, and Jessie saw that her forehead was bleeding profusely. Before anyone could say another word, the front door slammed shut. A loud locking sound followed. Jessie and Ryan turned in that direction, trying to discern what was going on. She caught a glimpse of movement in the window. Squinting, she saw what looked like Danielle Robertson scurrying toward the back of the house.

"It's her—Danielle Robertson," she said. "She ran down a back hallway and out of sight."

"I'm going in after her," Ryan said. "You help Ford and call for backup."

"Be careful," she warned. "There's probably one of those canisters in there somewhere."

"Was she wearing a mask?" he asked.

"I didn't see one, but that doesn't mean she's not putting it on right now."

"I'll be careful," he warned.

He kicked in the door, then disappeared inside. Once he was out of sight, Jessie rushed over to Sienna Ford, who was staring at her, blinking back blood from her bewildered eyes. Jessie yanked off her jacket as she got close.

"Sienna, my name is Jessie Hunt," she said quickly but calmly, "I work with the police. I'm here to help."

As she wrapped up Ford, who had begun to shiver, likely from a combination of shock, cold weather, and lack of clothing, she studied the wound on the woman's head. There was a deep gash where her forehead met her hairline. Jessie noticed more blood coming from the back of Ford's left hand, which appeared to be broken, and guessed that the injury was a defensive wound when Ford put up her hand to protect herself from a second blow.

"Listen," Jessie said sharply, grabbing the woman by the shoulders and staring hard at her, "I have to go help my partner in there, but I need you to give me some quick information first. You were attacked by Danielle Robertson, yes?"

"Yes," Ford said, her voice quavering.

"What weapon did she use?"

"A golf club. She hit me in the head with it as I was getting out of the tub. I managed to block her second swing and just started running."

"Was she wearing a gas mask when she attacked you?" Jessie pressed. "Did you rip one off her face?"

"No," Ford said, befuddled by the question.

"You were in your bathroom when the attack occurred?" Jessie confirmed.

Ford nodded.

"I feel like I'm going to throw up," she said weakly.

"I'm going to call for an ambulance," Jessie said, before pointing at her car. "In the meantime, I want you to go sit in that vehicle. It's unlocked. There are napkins in the glove compartment. Grab a bunch of them and press them against the wound on your head until help arrives. Do you understand?"

Ford nodded. Jessie again pointed her in the right direction, then turned and dashed toward the house. As she did, she called for backup, along with a hazmat unit and an ambulance. She unholstered her weapon and hurried through the door, then back in the direction she had seen Robertson go earlier.

As she made her way down the hallway, the relaxing sounds of Sade's "Paradise" could be heard throughout the house. Jessie tried to shut the music out as she fixed her attention on each open doorway along the hallway. A trail of blood drops on the hardwood floor led to the end of the hall, where she could hear voices other than the singer's.

She stepped into the last room at the end. It was a giant bedroom, Laid out on the bed were an elegant dress, along with a bra and panties.

Just beyond that were french doors leading to a bathroom. She made her way over.

When she got to the threshold, she took in the scene. Ryan was just in front of her, his weapon pointed at a closet door that was cracked slightly open. In that small slit, Jessie could see the face of Danielle Robertson, hidden behind a gas mask.

"How's it going in here?" she asked as nonchalantly as she could under the circumstances.

"Oh, hey, Honey," Ryan said, not turning around. "I was just talking to Danielle, who has requested that we call her Junior instead. She tells me that she has her finger on a remote control device that will activate a canister on the counter, releasing poison gas. I was letting her know that I thought that a bad idea."

Jessie glanced over at the vanity countertop and saw a familiar metal canister sitting just behind a bottle of mouthwash. It was less than five feet from her.

"Okay, good to know," Jessie said, trying to adopt the relaxed tone that her husband had cultivated. "Junior, how are you doing?"

"I've been better," the young woman shouted back, her voice muffled by the mask. "Things didn't go how I was hoping here."

"You were hoping to kill Sienna Ford," Jessie confirmed, "just like Avery Sinclair and the other clients we talked to you about this morning,"

"She had it coming," Danielle said with righteous certainty.

"What exactly did she do wrong?" Jessie wondered.

Danielle sighed heavily, as if explaining the enormity of the woman's crimes was a burden she could hardly bear.

"She was twisting her daughter into something ugly, just like all those other mothers were doing to their children," she said, the venom clear through the mask. "If I didn't do something to change things, all these kids were going to reach the point of no return, when they couldn't be salvaged. There's still time for them, but not with these women guiding them."

And all at once, Jessie understood. Her theory had only been half right. She thought that Danielle was targeting these women because they reminded her of the mean girls who had made her youth such a living hell. But this wasn't just about vengeance.

In her own unhinged way, Danielle thought she was helping, trying to prevent the cycle that had destroyed her childhood from repeating itself, with the very children she'd been tasked to help. Something had set her off, causing her to believe that she had to act now to prevent the kids she tutored from becoming someone else's torturer, if they weren't already.

"I get it," Jessie said.

"Sure you do," Danielle spat back sarcastically. "It all makes sense to you."

"No, I can't pretend to understand everything you've gone through, Junior," Jessie replied gently, "but I can imagine what led you to this place. Let me try. You were brutally, relentlessly attacked every day when you were young, by girls who probably grew up to be just like your clients. They pushed you to the brink, taunted you, saying you should end your own life. And when you finally fought back. you were the one who got punished. You were sent away. How am I doing so far?"

"So you got access to my records," Danielle scoffed. "Big deal, that doesn't mean you know me."

"No, of course not," Jessie conceded. "But I want to. I want to understand why a young woman who managed to overcome such obstacles and went on to such a promising future ended up in this position."

"Are you kidding?" Danielle shot back. "I'm rescuing these children. That's a pretty great position to be in. The world might not comprehend it right now, but history will."

"But who's going to rescue *you*?" Jessie asked. "Right now, you're locked in a prison of your own creation. You insist on being called by the hateful, insulting name those girls gave you all those years ago, rather than your own beautiful one. Instead of countering these mothers' insidious life lessons with your own empathetic ones, you've turned them into martyrs in the eyes of their kids, and you into the monster that can't be trusted. Surely that isn't what you wanted. And now you're threatening to kill two people who haven't wronged you or harmed any children."

"There's still time for you to do that," Danielle muttered.

"Maybe," Jessie told her, deciding now was as good a time as any to be completely honest. "I don't even know if I want to have children. Truthfully, I'm worried that I'd screw them up, that I'd pass on all my fears and failures to them. I have a lot of them. But one thing I know for sure is that if I was ever in that position, I'd try my damnedest to do right by them, to keep them safe, and to give them a brighter childhood than the one I had. And the man standing next to me isn't just my partner. He's my husband. And I know he feels the same way. Are you going to deny us that chance because your plan has fallen apart? Are you going to make our hearts stop beating in our chests because we got in the way of your attempt to turn children into orphans? Is that what you really want, Danielle?"

"Call me Junior!"

"I won't do that," Jessie said, ignoring Ryan, who visibly stiffened beside her. "That's a name given to you by people who don't deserve to have power over you anymore. You are not Junior or Chip. You're Danielle, a brilliant young woman who wants to do the right thing and made some terrible choices in the service of what she thought was an honorable path. There's still time to salvage the real Danielle. Come out of that closet. Turn yourself in. Tell your story at your trial. Let the world know what can happen when kids are put through what happened to you. You can be a cautionary tale and a source of hope for a different future. You can still make a difference in the world, maybe not in the way you thought, but still valuable, still meaningful. Please, Danielle."

Jessie stopped talking. She didn't know what to say. They waited silently for the woman's decision, both aware that if she made the wrong one, they likely couldn't get out of that bathroom in time to avoid the effects of the poison.

After what felt like an eternity, she pulled open the closet door and lifted her hands in the air. Neither Jessie nor Ryan made a move as they both saw that the remote control was still being held in her right hand.

She walked toward them, her heavy breathing fogging up the mask she wore, then stopped just feet away. She extended the hand with the remote control, her finger still on the trigger button. Then she gently rested the remote on the vanity countertop, pulled the mask off and dropped it on the ground. Her glasses were covered in condensation and her curly, sandy-colored hair was limp. She interlaced her hands behind her head and dropped down to her knees.

"I officially surrender," she said.

"That's good," Jessie told. "Now Detective Hernandez is going to handcuff you and read you your rights, okay?"

"Okay," Danielle said. "And just for the record, I think you might make a good mom."

"Why do you say that?" Jessie asked, bewildered that this was what was on the woman's mind.

"Because you're worried that you'll be a bad one," Danielle said. "A bad mom wouldn't care."

CHAPTER THIRTY

Jessie sat beside Ryan on the couch in Parker's Central Station office, listening as the captain updated them on the situation.

"Robertson will be arraigned on Monday morning," she said. "We'll keep her here over the weekend rather than send her to Twin Towers. I want her to have a full psych evaluation before she's put in gen pop over there."

"I think that's a good idea," Ryan said. "From what I could tell, she wouldn't do very well with the other inmates."

"Any word on how Sienna Ford is doing?" Jessie asked.

"Last I heard they had stitched up her head and were giving her CT scan," Parker said. "The doctors thought that she pretty clearly had a concussion, but they were checking for internal bleeding."

"I know how that goes," Jessie muttered.

"I know you do," Parker said. "I'm just glad that Robertson didn't get a swing in at you."

"Me too," Ryan said quietly.

"I think that by the end, she was more interested in getting my approval than bashing my head in," Jessie observed. "Maybe that's why she told us the location of the storage unit where she'd planted her two remaining canisters."

"Whatever works, Ms. Hunt," Parker said as there was a knock on her door.

"Come!" the captain barked.

Her administrative aide, Officer Shaniqua George, opened the door. "Can I borrow you for a moment, Captain?" she asked.

"I'll be right back," Parker said, stepping out of the office.

Once she was gone, Ryan leaned over and whispered in Jessie's ear.

"I've been intending to ask you, did you mean what you said to Danielle Robertson about kids?"

"What did I say exactly?" Jessie asked, only half-joking.

"That if you ever had them, you'd do everything you could to give them a better childhood than yours. It made it sound like you were considering the idea."

"Oh that," Jessie replied, with a dismissive wave. "I was just saying whatever I thought would get Danielle to give herself up."

"Sure you were, Ms. Hunt," he said, twinkle in his eye. "Sure you were."

Just then Parker returned to the room. "I have what I hope is some good news."

"Whatever it is, we'll take it," Ryan told her.

"I just heard from the folks handling the search for Hank Costabile," she said. "While we don't have a definitive lock on his location, we think we know where he is."

"Where?" Jessie asked.

"By the time we got someone on the Pacific Surfliner train in San Diego, he was gone, that is assuming he was ever actually on it. But we were able to use cameras at the train's last stop, Santa Fe Depot, to find someone matching his physical description—bald, thick-trunked, and wearing what Costabile was last seen in—leaving the station and getting in a cab. Our people ID'd the medallion number and tracked down the taxi driver. Apparently, the rider, who paid for his trip in cash, also matched Costabile's description. The driver said he drove the rider to the San Ysidro border crossing near Tijuana, where the passenger apparently said he was going to walk across the bridge and have himself a lost weekend. We're currently attempting to acquire U.S. Border Patrol footage from around the time of the drop-off. If it bears out, Ms. Hunt's theory—that he may have just gotten sick of being followed all day, every day and decided to give us the slip for a temporary reprieve from surveillance—might turn out to be the case."

"Do you buy that?" Ryan asked.

"Everything suggests that he may just be looking to get lost for a while," Parker acknowledged, "but I'll feel a lot more confident once I see the actual footage from the border crossing, with facial recognition verifying that it's him. Costabile had lots of friends in the department *and* among folks on the other side of the law. I'd imagine that some of them are bald and built like bulldozers too."

"And I'd also imagine that some of them feel like they owe him a favor," Jessie added.

Parker nodded in agreement.

"That's why, out of an abundance of caution, we'd like to leave that unit outside your house tonight," she said. "Same with the one at Kat Gentry's building. It might be overkill but I'd rather not take the chance."

"I think we're both okay with all that, right?" Ryan said, looking at Jessie.

She nodded. "If you're going all out," she said, "you may want to have a unit accompany us to our last stop of the evening."

"Where is that?" Parker asked.

"I'm going to see Mark Haddonfield at Twin Towers," Jessie said.

The captain shook her head in disapproval.

"I was hoping you'd change your mind about that," she said. "Don't you worry that you're just feeding into his delusions of grandeur by meeting with him in person?"

"After what happened to Janice Lemmon, I have to do something to make this stop," Jessie said. "The doctors say that she'll be okay, but that doesn't change anything. People are using Haddonfield's manifesto as a guidebook to go after the folks I care about. And if playing to his ego keeps them safe, then it's a trade-off I'm willing to make."

"Are you good with this?" Parker asked Ryan.

"Captain," he replied, sounding amused, "I would think that by now, you'd know it's not my call."

"All right," Parker said, despite her lack of enthusiasm. "Give me a minute to coordinate with Sergeant Crowley. He's on dispatch duty tonight. He'll have a squad car accompany you there."

"Better hurry," Jessie said. "I'm heading over there now. And once that's done I'm checking in on my sister and my best friend. As far as I'm concerned, my work day is officially over."

"And you think Haddonfield's delusional?" Ryan cracked.

"What does that mean?" Jessie asked.

"I've known you a long time, Jessie Hunt. Your work day is never officially over."

CHAPTER THIRTY ONE

Mark Haddonfield knew something was up.

As the guard escorted him down the hallway, both his wrists and ankles manacled, he initially thought that he was going to the Twin Towers Correctional Facility visiting room. But it was 6:35, well after visiting hours. Sure enough, they passed by the darkened room without stopping.

The guard finally had him come to a halt outside a conference room further down the hall. Mark was familiar with it. The room was typically used for inmates who were meeting with lawyers in preparation for a court proceeding. His trial was coming up soon, but he was still surprised. His lawyer hadn't shown much of a predilection for working extra hours.

He stood at the door for a couple of minutes, waiting quietly and studying himself in the glass window. Even though he'd been in jail for three months now, he didn't think he looked much different than before. He was still a tall, skinny, twenty-one-year-old former college student with pale skin, curly blond hair, and glasses.

Eventually, a second guard stepped out of the conference room and held the door open for him. He entered slowly. When he saw who was seated at the table, he didn't know how to react.

Jessie Hunt was staring back at him in all her glory. Her brown hair was tied back in a ponytail. She wore a navy sweater and tan slacks. She looked tired to him, as if she hadn't gotten any sleep last night. Despite that, she was still as beautiful in real life as she was in his dreams. He found himself both elated to see her and worried for her welfare.

"Ms. Hunt," he said, unable to hold back a smile, "I can honestly say that I didn't expect to see you tonight."

She shrugged at him, clearly not as enthused to be here as he was.

"I'm not as full of surprises as you, but I try," she said, her voice as weary-sounding as she looked. "Have a seat."

One of the guards motioned for him to sit in the chair across from her that was bolted to the ground.

"To what do I owe the honor?" he asked.

She sighed heavily, as if not entirely certain that she wanted to answer. Finally, she seemed to almost physically shake off whatever reservations she had. The air of exhaustion enveloping her disappeared, and she stared at him with her eyes focused, her body taut.

"I have a proposition for you," she told him, leaning forward.

Mark tried to act cool but found it impossible to pull off.

"Color me intrigued," he said eagerly. "Please go on."

"I don't know how much information you have access to in here, but I wanted to share a few updates," she told him. "Since your manifesto was released a month ago, two people close to me have suffered. My friend Kat Gentry's fiancé was murdered by a fan of yours who was trying to kill her. And just today, Dr. Janice Lemmon was attacked. Luckily, she survived and is recovering well."

Mark held up his manacled palms to her. "What can I tell you?" he said. "I'd like to say I'm sorry to hear that, but it would be disingenuous. This is exactly what I was hoping for, after all."

"I realize that," she said. "That's why I'm here. I need for these attacks to stop. I need you to make them stop."

"Why would I do that?" he asked.

"Because of my proposition," she told him. "Here's my offer, and it's not open to negotiation."

"Look at you, all business," he couldn't help but tease.

She ignored the comment and pressed ahead.

"You disavow the manifesto, publicly, in a video that will be posted on the internet," she said. "You tell your followers that your mission has been accomplished and that any further attacks on me or others in my orbit would be in contravention of your wishes. In exchange, I will allow you to work with me on cases."

Mark waited several seconds to see if she would tell him she was joking. When she didn't, he replied.

"Wait," he said, still not sure he'd heard her correctly, "what does that mean exactly?"

"It means that you would finally get what you wanted, Mark: to be my protégé. Obviously, there would be limits. You're about to go on trial for multiple murders. You will likely spend the rest of your life in prison. And I would still be working a full-time job as a profiler. But I would be willing to periodically come to you with cases, ones where I thought that your skills and insight could be particularly useful."

"That's interesting," he conceded.

"We're not talking weekly visits here, Mark, especially considering that after you're convicted, you might be sent to a prison some distance from L.A. But I'd be willing to commit to working with you, say, monthly. That would allow you to make a real difference, even behind bars. You would get the appropriate recognition for your efforts. You could help save lives rather than take them. And who knows, maybe your help could ultimately prove so valuable that you're moved to a better prison, where you'd get more perks and not have to worry about…accidents." she said nodding at his hands.

It was reference to the broken middle finger on his left hand and the broken ring finger on his right, both courtesy of his cellmate, Oscar, who didn't like it when he got too chatty.

"How do I know I can trust you?" he asked. "How can I be sure that once I make the video, you won't just forget about me?"

"Do I strike you as the kind of person who welches on promises, Mark?" she asked, sounding offended. "If I commit to working with you, then I will hold up my end of the bargain. But you need to do the same thing. If I agree to invest in your potential, and then someone I care about is harmed in any way by one of your followers, then the deal is off for good. So you need to be damn convincing in that video. What do you say?"

She leaned back and folded her arms. He studied her face. She didn't appear to be lying. Her eyes weren't darting, and her brow wasn't furrowed. And why would she lie? It served no purpose for her. If she didn't follow through, word would get out, destroying her credibility.

"Can I think about it for a second?" he asked.

"Of course," she said. "Take all the time you need."

"He has to be back in his cell in five minutes," the guard by the door noted.

"Okay, then take about three minutes," she said, correcting herself.

Mark could hear the voice whispering off to the side. He tried not to look in that direction. He didn't want to give away his advisor's presence.

You can't trust her, his Jessie said, her lips brushing his ear gently. *She'll use you and betray you. Just like she betrayed you before, when she wouldn't let you in her class, when she stopped teaching at the university without warning. She can't be trusted.*

He was usually inclined to follow her advice. This version of Jessie had been with him for months, guiding him, warning him about the dangers he faced as he pursued his mission of vengeance. She'd been with him as he planned his murders, and she had stayed by his side in his cell.

But now he couldn't help but question her motives. Was she jealous of Jessie Hunt, sitting across from him, finally willing to bury the hatchet? Did she fear that she would be replaced? Was she truly looking out for him, or was she more concerned with her own well-being?"

You know that's not it, she hissed quietly. *My interests are your interests, always. We're one and the same.*

Mark wanted to reply out loud, but he knew that Jessie Hunt and the guards in the room would find that odd. Jessie Hunt had already caught him talking to his Jessie once and asked about his "imaginary friend." He couldn't have that again. So he simply responded though thoughts. His Jessie would hear them, after all.

Jessie Hunt has to know that if she violates this agreement, if she betrays me, then I will sic my rabid dogs on her again. This is a sincere offer. You know it is. I'll say on alert, just as you will. But I have to take it.

His Jessie, still hovering next to him, didn't respond. Mark knew she wasn't happy. But she would come to accept this.

"We have a deal," he said.

"Wonderful," Jessie said from across the table. "I'll coordinate the video shoot with the warden and the prosecutor's office. If everything moves quickly, you and I will be working together very soon."

She stood up, grabbed her coat, and headed for the door. Just before leaving, she turned back. "I think this is the beginning of, well maybe not a beautiful friendship, but at the very least, a productive relationship."

Mark got the feeling that she was paraphrasing something, perhaps a movie or a book, but he didn't get the reference. It didn't matter anyway. He could always ask her about it the next time he saw her as they laid the groundwork to team up and start solving cases. He felt positively giddy as the guard instructed him to stand up, leave the room, and shuffle back toward the cells.

As he made his way down the hallway, he saw the other guard at the end of the hall, muttering to someone on his cell phone. Mark couldn't totally make out what he was saying, but as he got closer, he did hear the words "leaving now.... outside in five... dark blue sweater."

Mark stared at the man, whose quiet tone and furtive demeanor suggested he was up to no good.

"Who are you talking to?" he demanded. "What's that about?"

The guard looked at him as he hung up and put the phone in his pocket. Then, without warning, he punched Mark in the gut. He dropped to his knees, coughing, gasping for breath.

"None of your business," the guard growled, before turning to the other guard. "Drag him back if you have to."

As the other guard ripped him to his feet and yanked him down the hall, Mark wasn't concerned for his own welfare. All he could think was one thing: Jessie Hunt was in danger and there was nothing he could do about it.

CHAPTER THIRTY TWO

Jessie walked out of the main doors of Twin Towers and headed down the long walking path toward the street. The temperature had dropped precipitously after the sun set two hours ago, and she quickly zipped up her jacket, pulled the hood over her head, and texted Ryan.

Leaving Twin Towers now. Headed back to the car. See you in two minutes.

His response came quickly.

Got tired of sitting around. Went around the block to that burrito place. Got your favorite. Headed back now. If I'm not there when you get to the sidewalk, hang out by the officers in the squad car.

Okay. See you soon, she typed, then put her phone away before shoving her hands deep in her pockets to protect against the chill. As she approached the street, she looked around for the squad car with the officers that Parker had the dispatch sergeant assign to her. She didn't immediately see them.

She became briefly concerned until she registered the cacophony of sirens coming from about six blocks away. Something was clearly going on, and if it was serious enough, they'd likely have been called away from some boring protection duty to help out. Jessie knew where she stood in the pecking order.

She reached the end of the pathway and turned left onto the sidewalk, walking along the chain link fence and looking for a free spot between cars where Ryan could pull in and pick her up when he returned. As a precaution, with the squad car gone, she reached down to undo the snap on her gun holster. Suddenly, she froze in place.

She was an idiot. She remembered turning the weapon in to the guard at the gun locker window when she went to see Haddonfield. Not only that, but her taser too. But when she left, she was so excited to finally be on a path to keeping her loved ones safe, that she had forgotten about retrieving them. And now that she thought about it, she recalled that the guard wasn't there to remind her when she walked past him. He must have been on a break. Now, she had to go all the way back to retrieve it.

Jessie turned around. That's when she saw him. Coming toward her on the sidewalk, about thirty yards away, was a hulking man in a hoodie. His head was down, focused on the ground. Even if he'd been looking up, it was much too dark to see his face. He was walking slowly but with a sense of purpose. He didn't seem to have realized she'd turned his way.

As casually as she could, Jessie turned on her heel and headed back in the direction she'd just come from, away from him. She reminded herself not to jump to conclusions. It could just be some guy, any guy.

But something deep in her gut told her who it was. She forced herself to breathe as she continued walking, moving at a brisk pace but not breaking into a run. She considered pulling out her phone to call or text Ryan but feared that would reveal to the hoodie guy that she was aware of his presence.

Instead, she just kept walking. As she passed a pickup truck, she glanced in its sideview mirror. It was clear that the man behind her was closer now and moving fast. She guessed that he'd made up half the distance between them since she first turned around.

She picked up pace to get to the next car. As she glanced in its mirror, she saw something that made her blood run cold. The man, now less than ten paces behind her, was reaching for something in his pocket. In the dim glow of the streetlight, the thing flashed. It was a knife.

Jessie forced herself to think. She was alone. She had no weapon. And a man she was almost positive was Hank Costabile was coming up behind her with a knife. Maybe if she had the element of surprise, she could get in a quick kick or blow and make a run for it. But he was ready for her. He was stronger than her. He was armed. And he was almost on her.

She passed by a white van, hoping to get one last bit of help from its mirror when she heard the footsteps behind her break into a run. Without looking back, she did the same, passing by the hood of the van and then darting in front of it. Staying low but not stopping, she rushed around to the street and the passenger side of the van and peeked through the window. The man had stopped by the driver's side door, lingering there.

It occurred to her that he didn't know she was unarmed and was proceeding with caution in case she was waiting in front of the van, gun drawn, ready to fire. She took advantage of his uncertainty and made her way to the back of the van, quickly but quietly.

She was near the rear doors of the van when he stepped out into the street in front of the hood. Apparently, he'd gotten over his concern about being shot and checked, finding that she wasn't there. Now, he had a clear path to her, and she was without a van to hide behind. The vehicle parked behind the van was a Subaru station wagon that offered nothing in the way of concealment.

The man rushed at her. She turned around and was about to bolt down the street when she changed her mind. She might be faster than the guy over a long distance, but he would catch her in a sprint. She had to change the dynamic.

So rather than run she took two huge steps and leapt up onto the hood of the Subaru. Then, without pausing, she scrambled up to the roof of the car and spun around. The man stopped in front of the hood of the car, apparently debating his next move.

Then, slowly, he pulled off his hoodie. Hank Costabile stood in front of her, a nasty smile on his face, a switchblade in his hand, flickering in the streetlight.

"Hi, Jessie," he snarled. "It's been a minute."

"Not long enough," she shot back with far more arrogance than she felt.

"I'm guessing you don't have your gun, or you'd have shot me by now," he noted.

"There's still time for you to turn around and go home," she said. "You haven't committed any crimes yet, at least not since you got out of prison."

"But I'm about to," he told her. "You didn't really think I could just let things lie, did you? Or that I'd actually run off to Tijuana?"

"No," she told him, hoping to delay the inevitable. "I figured you found some lookalike lackey to take your place."

She unzipped her jacket and took it off. It wasn't much, but it was the only thing at her disposal. Maybe she could whip it at him to keep him at bay, or even knock the knife out of his hand.

"You figured right," he said as he clambered up onto the hood of the Subaru, denting it repeatedly. "There are lots of folks who want to help me, some of them in your own police station. They're all tired of a mouthy bitch like you messing things up for the rest of us."

"Such a gentleman," she said. "I would have thought you'd have learned some manners in prison, but it looks like you're just the same old human bowling ball."

Jessie had made her decision. She couldn't outrun this guy. And she couldn't outfight him. But maybe she could outthink him. The very fact that Costabile was putting his freedom at risk to come after her was proof that he was fueled by rage more than brains. Maybe she could get him so angry that he made a mistake.

"Yeah, well, this human bowling ball is about to gut you like a fish."

"I doubt it," she said. "If you try to climb up here with me, you'll probably fall through the roof, big boy."

"Let's find out," he spat, moving forward on the hood.

She flicked the jacket at him like a whip, making him lose his balance slightly, but not enough to fall off the car. As he walked up the windshield, she retreated to the back of the roof. Maybe he really would be heavy enough to crash through the thing if he got up there with her. But she wasn't holding her breath.

Jessie was running out of ideas, and the sound of a blaring car horn in the distance wasn't helping her concentrate. Costabile was on the roof with her now and though he looked a little unsteady on his feet, he was in no danger of caving the thing in.

The honking behind them got louder and closer. Jessie stole a glance back. What she saw made her heart sing. Ryan was driving toward them—fast—and waving his arm at her wildly. She looked back at Costabile and realized that her husband and partner wouldn't get there in time. There just wasn't enough of it for him to pull over and get off a good shot before Costabile did his work.

"Looks like your time has come," the former cop told her, a mad grimace on his face. He was now in lunging distance, gripping the knife tightly.

Jessie heard the honk again and pictured Ryan behind her, still waving wildly. And in a flash, she realized that hadn't been waving wildly at all. He was swinging his arm backward, telling her to move in that direction. Now she understood. He was telling her to jump.

Without hesitation, she grabbed her jacket in both hands and flung it at Costabile's face. As he swiped at it with the knife, she turned, jumped down to the trunk of the Subaru and leapt onto the hood of the Honda Civic right behind it. She landed hard on her knees but ignored the pain and spun around.

Costabile had won his battle with her jacket and was leaping down onto the Subaru's trunk. But just as his feet landed, the hood of Ryan's car slammed into the trunk. Costabile was going forward one moment and the next he was slingshot back into the air.

Jessie watched him fly thirty feet before slamming into the chain link fence next to the sidewalk along the perimeter of the Twin Towers. The fence caught him like a catcher's mitt before he fell to the sidewalk.

Ryan leapt out of the driver's seat and looked over at Jessie.

"Are you okay?" he said.

"I think so."

"Stay there," he instructed as he dashed between the cars and toward Costabile.

The man saw him coming and tried to get to his feet. Jessie was amazed that he could move at all. As he used the fence to pull himself up, Jessie noted that his right leg was bent the wrong way at the knee. Seemingly oblivious, he snatched up the knife, which was resting beside him on the sidewalk.

"I wanted her," he grunted as Ryan came toward him, "But you'll do just as well."

When Ryan was close enough, Costabile swung wildly at him with the blade, but Ryan blocked it easily before slamming the man up against the fence with his left forearm, pinning his neck. With his right hand, he grabbed Costabile's right hand, which still clutched the knife, and snapped it at the wrist.

Costabile yelped in pain as the knife dropped from his hand, which now dangled uselessly at his side. With the former sergeant still pinned against the fence, Ryan reared back and punched him in the face. Then he did it again. And again. And again.

Costabile's body slumped but Ryan held him up with his free hand while he pummeled him relentless with his right. Eventually the sheer weight of the man was too much to keep upright, and he toppled to the ground, face-first.

Ryan knelt down and flipped him over. He put his palm on the top of Costabile's head to keep him steady, then resumed punching him in the face. Jessie lost count of the blows as she watched her husband turn the man into a pulpy mess.

She realized that unless she did something, he was going to kill Costabile with his bare hands. Some dark part of her wanted him to keep going, wanted him to smash his fist through the back of the man's skull. But she couldn't let it happen, not because of anything particularly decent in her. She had to stop him because Ryan was a cop, not a killer, and he'd never be able to live with himself if he crossed that line.

"Ryan, stop!" she yelled.

But he didn't. Jessie wasn't even sure he had heard her over the sounds of his fist smashing against the crunching bones in Costabile's face. She couldn't see his eyes but imagined the frenzied rage in them as he shut everything else out. She was too far away to restrain him. By the time she got to them, Costabile would be a lifeless corpse.

"Ryan, you have to stop!" she screamed again, her voice piercing the darkness.

Her husband's blood-drenched fist froze in mid-air.

"Stop," she repeated. "It's enough. Arrest him. Cuff him. But don't kill him. That's not who you are."

Ryan turned and looked at her, his eyes filled with fury.

"How can we be sure that he won't get out again?" he pleaded through gasps for air, "that he won't come after you again?"

"He's not ever getting out again," she promised him. "And if he does, I'll be the one to take him out."

Ryan's fist still hovered in the air for a few seconds before he finally relented. Without a word, he pulled out his handcuffs, rolled the barely conscious Costabile onto his stomach, and cuffed his hands behind his back. As he began reading the former police sergeant his rights, Jessie slumped back on the hood of the car.

She stared at Costabile, whose ruined mouth was covered in bloody saliva bubbles, making sure to lock the image in her brain. She felt no pity for him. It was only her love for Ryan—for his reputation and his future—that made her stop him.

But if she and Costabile ever met on a dark street again, she would pick up where Ryan left off. Only *she* wouldn't stop. She wouldn't even try to. She knew what she was capable of.

After all, Jessie Hunt was the daughter of a serial killer. She'd learned to harness the dark impulses he'd passed down to her into something productive, something that helped society. She'd turned her family's taste for vengeance into a thirst for justice.

But if she let it, that lust for retribution could turn on a dime. It was in her blood. And it was always there, hibernating somewhere deep inside of her.

All she had to do was let it out.

NOW AVAILABLE!

THE PERFECT POISE
(A Jessie Hunt Psychological Suspense Thriller—Book Thirty-Four)

In the elite world of the ultra-ultra rich, women are turning up dead in their mansions, behind their massive gates, in places where nothing should ever go wrong. Jessie is shocked at the wealth of this world, at how dysfunctional the seemingly-perfect are, and at what lengths they will go to cover up their past, and their lies….

"A masterpiece of thriller and mystery."
—Books and Movie Reviews, Roberto Mattos (re Once Gone)

THE PERFECT POISE is book #34 in a new psychological suspense series by bestselling author Blake Pierce, which begins with *The Perfect Wife*, a #1 bestseller (and free download) with over 5,000 five-star ratings and 1,000 five-star reviews.

A fast-paced psychological suspense thriller with unforgettable characters and heart-pounding suspense, the JESSIE HUNT series is a riveting new series that will leave you turning pages late into the night.

Future books in the series are also available.

"An edge of your seat thriller in a new series that keeps you turning pages! ...So many twists, turns and red herrings… I can't wait to see what happens next."
—Reader review (Her Last Wish)

"A strong, complex story about two FBI agents trying to stop a serial killer. If you want an author to capture your attention and have you guessing, yet trying to put the pieces together, Pierce is your author!"
—Reader review (Her Last Wish)

"A typical Blake Pierce twisting, turning, roller coaster ride suspense thriller. Will have you turning the pages to the last sentence of the last chapter!!!"

—Reader review (City of Prey)

"Right from the start we have an unusual protagonist that I haven't seen done in this genre before. The action is nonstop… A very atmospheric novel that will keep you turning pages well into the wee hours."
—Reader review (City of Prey)

"Everything that I look for in a book… a great plot, interesting characters, and grabs your interest right away. The book moves along at a breakneck pace and stays that way until the end. Now on go I to book two!"
—Reader review (Girl, Alone)

"Exciting, heart pounding, edge of your seat book… a must read for mystery and suspense readers!"
—Reader review (Girl, Alone)

Blake Pierce

Blake Pierce is the USA Today bestselling author of the RILEY PAGE mystery series, which includes seventeen books. Blake Pierce is also the author of the MACKENZIE WHITE mystery series, comprising fourteen books; of the AVERY BLACK mystery series, comprising six books; of the KERI LOCKE mystery series, comprising five books; of the MAKING OF RILEY PAIGE mystery series, comprising six books; of the KATE WISE mystery series, comprising seven books; of the CHLOE FINE psychological suspense mystery, comprising six books; of the JESSIE HUNT psychological suspense thriller series, comprising thirty-eight books (and counting); of the AU PAIR psychological suspense thriller series, comprising three books; of the ZOE PRIME mystery series, comprising six books; of the ADELE SHARP mystery series, comprising sixteen books, of the EUROPEAN VOYAGE cozy mystery series, comprising six books; of the LAURA FROST FBI suspense thriller, comprising eleven books; of the ELLA DARK FBI suspense thriller, comprising twenty-one books (and counting); of the A YEAR IN EUROPE cozy mystery series, comprising nine books, of the AVA GOLD mystery series, comprising six books; of the RACHEL GIFT mystery series, comprising fifteen books (and counting); of the VALERIE LAW mystery series, comprising nine books; of the PAIGE KING mystery series, comprising eight books; of the MAY MOORE mystery series, comprising eleven books; of the CORA SHIELDS mystery series, comprising eight books; of the NICKY LYONS mystery series, comprising eight books, of the CAMI LARK mystery series, comprising ten books; of the AMBER YOUNG mystery series, comprising eight books; of the DAISY FORTUNE mystery series, comprising five books; of the FIONA RED mystery series, comprising thirteen books (and counting); of the FAITH BOLD mystery series, comprising seventeen books (and counting); of the JULIETTE HART mystery series, comprising five books; of the MORGAN CROSS mystery series, comprising thirteen books (and counting); of the FINN WRIGHT mystery series, comprising seven books (and counting); of the SHEILA STONE suspense thriller series, comprising eight books (and counting); of the RACHEL BLACKWOOD suspense thriller series, comprising eight books (and counting); and of the new THE GOVERNESS psychological suspense thriller series, comprising five books (and counting).

An avid reader and lifelong fan of the mystery and thriller genres, Blake loves to hear from you, so please feel free to visit www.blakepierceauthor.com to learn more and stay in touch.

BOOKS BY BLAKE PIERCE

THE GOVERNESS PSYCHOLOGICAL SUSPENSE
ONE LAST LIE (Book #1)
ONE LAST SMILE (Book #2)
ONE LAST BREATH (Book #3)
ONE LAST GOODBYE (Book #4)
ONE LAST SECRET (Book #5)

RACHEL BLACKWOOD SUSPENSE THRILLER
NOT THIS WAY (Book #1)
NOT THIS TIME (Book #2)
NOT THIS CLOSE (Book #3)
NOT THIS ROAD (Book #4)
NOT THIS LATE (Book #5)
NOT THIS NIGHT (Book #6)
NOT THIS PLACE (Book #7)
NOT THIS SOON (Book #8)

SHEILA STONE SUSPENSE THRILLER
SILENT GIRL (Book #1)
SILENT TRAIL (Book #2)
SILENT NIGHT (Book #3)
SILENT HOUSE (Book #4)
SILENT SCREAM (Book #5)
SILENT PREY (Book #6)
SILENT RITUAL (Book #7)
SILENT PRAYER (Book #8)

FINN WRIGHT MYSTERY SERIES
WHEN YOU'RE MINE (Book #1)
WHEN YOU'RE SAFE (Book #2)
WHEN YOU'RE CLOSE (Book #3)
WHEN YOU'RE SLEEPING (Book #4)
WHEN YOU'RE SANE (Book #5)
WHEN YOU'RE SILENT (Book #6)
WHEN YOU'RE GONE (Book #7)

MORGAN CROSS MYSTERY SERIES
FOR YOU (Book #1)
FOR RAGE (Book #2)
FOR LUST (Book #3)
FOR WRATH (Book #4)
FOREVER (Book #5)
FOR US (Book #6)
FOR NOW (Book #7)
FOR ONCE (Book #8)
FOR ETERNITY (Book #9)
FORLORN (Book #10)
FOR SILENCE (Book #11)
FORBIDDEN (Book #12)
FOR FEAR (Book #13)
FORSAKEN (Book #14)

JULIETTE HART MYSTERY SERIES
NOTHING TO FEAR (Book #1)
NOTHING THERE (Book #2)
NOTHING WATCHING (Book #3)
NOTHING HIDING (Book #4)
NOTHING LEFT (Book #5)

FAITH BOLD MYSTERY SERIES
SO LONG (Book #1)
SO COLD (Book #2)
SO SCARED (Book #3)
SO NORMAL (Book #4)
SO FAR GONE (Book #5)
SO LOST (Book #6)
SO ALONE (Book #7)
SO FORGOTTEN (Book #8)
SO INSANE (Book #9)
SO SMITTEN (Book #10)
SO SIMPLE (Book #11)
SO BROKEN (Book #12)
SO CRUEL (Book #13)
SO HAUNTED (Book #14)
SO SILENT (Book #15)

SO BLEAK (Book #16)
SO HOLLOW (Book #17)

FIONA RED MYSTERY SERIES
LET HER GO (Book #1)
LET HER BE (Book #2)
LET HER HOPE (Book #3)
LET HER WISH (Book #4)
LET HER LIVE (Book #5)
LET HER RUN (Book #6)
LET HER HIDE (Book #7)
LET HER BELIEVE (Book #8)
LET HER FORGET (Book #9)
LET HER TRY (Book #10)
LET HER PLAY (Book #11)
LET HER VANISH (Book #12)
LET HER FADE (Book #13)

DAISY FORTUNE MYSTERY SERIES
NEED YOU (Book #1)
CLAIM YOU (Book #2)
CRAVE YOU (Book #3)
CHOOSE YOU (Book #4)
CHASE YOU (Book #5)

AMBER YOUNG MYSTERY SERIES
ABSENT PITY (Book #1)
ABSENT REMORSE (Book #2)
ABSENT FEELING (Book #3)
ABSENT MERCY (Book #4)
ABSENT REASON (Book #5)
ABSENT SANITY (Book #6)
ABSENT LIFE (Book #7)
ABSENT HUMANITY (Book #8)

CAMI LARK MYSTERY SERIES
JUST ME (Book #1)
JUST OUTSIDE (Book #2)
JUST RIGHT (Book #3)
JUST FORGET (Book #4)

JUST ONCE (Book #5)
JUST HIDE (Book #6)
JUST NOW (Book #7)
JUST HOPE (Book #8)
JUST LEAVE (Book #9)
JUST TONIGHT (Book #10)

NICKY LYONS MYSTERY SERIES
ALL MINE (Book #1)
ALL HIS (Book #2)
ALL HE SEES (Book #3)
ALL ALONE (Book #4)
ALL FOR ONE (Book #5)
ALL HE TAKES (Book #6)
ALL FOR ME (Book #7)
ALL IN (Book #8)

CORA SHIELDS MYSTERY SERIES
UNDONE (Book #1)
UNWANTED (Book #2)
UNHINGED (Book #3)
UNSAID (Book #4)
UNGLUED (Book #5)
UNSTABLE (Book #6)
UNKNOWN (Book #7)
UNAWARE (Book #8)

MAY MOORE SUSPENSE THRILLER
NEVER RUN (Book #1)
NEVER TELL (Book #2)
NEVER LIVE (Book #3)
NEVER HIDE (Book #4)
NEVER FORGIVE (Book #5)
NEVER AGAIN (Book #6)
NEVER LOOK BACK (Book #7)
NEVER FORGET (Book #8)
NEVER LET GO (Book #9)
NEVER PRETEND (Book #10)
NEVER HESITATE (Book #11)

PAIGE KING MYSTERY SERIES
THE GIRL HE PINED (Book #1)
THE GIRL HE CHOSE (Book #2)
THE GIRL HE TOOK (Book #3)
THE GIRL HE WISHED (Book #4)
THE GIRL HE CROWNED (Book #5)
THE GIRL HE WATCHED (Book #6)
THE GIRL HE WANTED (Book #7)
THE GIRL HE CLAIMED (Book #8)

VALERIE LAW MYSTERY SERIES
NO MERCY (Book #1)
NO PITY (Book #2)
NO FEAR (Book #3)
NO SLEEP (Book #4)
NO QUARTER (Book #5)
NO CHANCE (Book #6)
NO REFUGE (Book #7)
NO GRACE (Book #8)
NO ESCAPE (Book #9)

RACHEL GIFT MYSTERY SERIES
HER LAST WISH (Book #1)
HER LAST CHANCE (Book #2)
HER LAST HOPE (Book #3)
HER LAST FEAR (Book #4)
HER LAST CHOICE (Book #5)
HER LAST BREATH (Book #6)
HER LAST MISTAKE (Book #7)
HER LAST DESIRE (Book #8)
HER LAST REGRET (Book #9)
HER LAST HOUR (Book #10)
HER LAST SHOT (Book #11)
HER LAST PRAYER (Book #12)
HER LAST LIE (Book #13)
HER LAST WHISPER (Book #14)
HER LAST SECRET (Book #15)

AVA GOLD MYSTERY SERIES
CITY OF PREY (Book #1)

CITY OF FEAR (Book #2)
CITY OF BONES (Book #3)
CITY OF GHOSTS (Book #4)
CITY OF DEATH (Book #5)
CITY OF VICE (Book #6)

A YEAR IN EUROPE
A MURDER IN PARIS (Book #1)
DEATH IN FLORENCE (Book #2)
VENGEANCE IN VIENNA (Book #3)
A FATALITY IN SPAIN (Book #4)

ELLA DARK FBI SUSPENSE THRILLER
GIRL, ALONE (Book #1)
GIRL, TAKEN (Book #2)
GIRL, HUNTED (Book #3)
GIRL, SILENCED (Book #4)
GIRL, VANISHED (Book 5)
GIRL ERASED (Book #6)
GIRL, FORSAKEN (Book #7)
GIRL, TRAPPED (Book #8)
GIRL, EXPENDABLE (Book #9)
GIRL, ESCAPED (Book #10)
GIRL, HIS (Book #11)
GIRL, LURED (Book #12)
GIRL, MISSING (Book #13)
GIRL, UNKNOWN (Book #14)
GIRL, DECEIVED (Book #15)
GIRL, FORLORN (Book #16)
GIRL, REMADE (Book #17)
GIRL, BETRAYED (Book #18)
GIRL, BOUND (Book #19)
GIRL, REFORMED (Book #20)
GIRL, REBORN (Book #21)

LAURA FROST FBI SUSPENSE THRILLER
ALREADY GONE (Book #1)
ALREADY SEEN (Book #2)
ALREADY TRAPPED (Book #3)
ALREADY MISSING (Book #4)

ALREADY DEAD (Book #5)
ALREADY TAKEN (Book #6)
ALREADY CHOSEN (Book #7)
ALREADY LOST (Book #8)
ALREADY HIS (Book #9)
ALREADY LURED (Book #10)
ALREADY COLD (Book #11)

EUROPEAN VOYAGE COZY MYSTERY SERIES
MURDER (AND BAKLAVA) (Book #1)
DEATH (AND APPLE STRUDEL) (Book #2)
CRIME (AND LAGER) (Book #3)
MISFORTUNE (AND GOUDA) (Book #4)
CALAMITY (AND A DANISH) (Book #5)
MAYHEM (AND HERRING) (Book #6)

ADELE SHARP MYSTERY SERIES
LEFT TO DIE (Book #1)
LEFT TO RUN (Book #2)
LEFT TO HIDE (Book #3)
LEFT TO KILL (Book #4)
LEFT TO MURDER (Book #5)
LEFT TO ENVY (Book #6)
LEFT TO LAPSE (Book #7)
LEFT TO VANISH (Book #8)
LEFT TO HUNT (Book #9)
LEFT TO FEAR (Book #10)
LEFT TO PREY (Book #11)
LEFT TO LURE (Book #12)
LEFT TO CRAVE (Book #13)
LEFT TO LOATHE (Book #14)
LEFT TO HARM (Book #15)
LEFT TO RUIN (Book #16)

THE AU PAIR SERIES
ALMOST GONE (Book#1)
ALMOST LOST (Book #2)
ALMOST DEAD (Book #3)

ZOE PRIME MYSTERY SERIES

FACE OF DEATH (Book#1)
FACE OF MURDER (Book #2)
FACE OF FEAR (Book #3)
FACE OF MADNESS (Book #4)
FACE OF FURY (Book #5)
FACE OF DARKNESS (Book #6)

A JESSIE HUNT PSYCHOLOGICAL SUSPENSE SERIES
THE PERFECT WIFE (Book #1)
THE PERFECT BLOCK (Book #2)
THE PERFECT HOUSE (Book #3)
THE PERFECT SMILE (Book #4)
THE PERFECT LIE (Book #5)
THE PERFECT LOOK (Book #6)
THE PERFECT AFFAIR (Book #7)
THE PERFECT ALIBI (Book #8)
THE PERFECT NEIGHBOR (Book #9)
THE PERFECT DISGUISE (Book #10)
THE PERFECT SECRET (Book #11)
THE PERFECT FAÇADE (Book #12)
THE PERFECT IMPRESSION (Book #13)
THE PERFECT DECEIT (Book #14)
THE PERFECT MISTRESS (Book #15)
THE PERFECT IMAGE (Book #16)
THE PERFECT VEIL (Book #17)
THE PERFECT INDISCRETION (Book #18)
THE PERFECT RUMOR (Book #19)
THE PERFECT COUPLE (Book #20)
THE PERFECT MURDER (Book #21)
THE PERFECT HUSBAND (Book #22)
THE PERFECT SCANDAL (Book #23)
THE PERFECT MASK (Book #24)
THE PERFECT RUSE (Book #25)
THE PERFECT VENEER (Book #26)
THE PERFECT PEOPLE (Book #27)
THE PERFECT WITNESS (Book #28)
THE PERFECT APPEARANCE (Book #29)
THE PERFECT TRAP (Book #30)
THE PERFECT EXPRESSION (Book #31)
THE PERFECT ACCOMPLICE (Book #32)

THE PERFECT SHOW (Book #33)
THE PERFECT POISE (Book #34)
THE PERFECT CROWD (Book #35)
THE PERFECT CRIME (Book #36)
THE PERFECT PREY (Book #37)
THE PERFECT BETRAYAL (Book #38)

CHLOE FINE PSYCHOLOGICAL SUSPENSE SERIES
NEXT DOOR (Book #1)
A NEIGHBOR'S LIE (Book #2)
CUL DE SAC (Book #3)
SILENT NEIGHBOR (Book #4)
HOMECOMING (Book #5)
TINTED WINDOWS (Book #6)

KATE WISE MYSTERY SERIES
IF SHE KNEW (Book #1)
IF SHE SAW (Book #2)
IF SHE RAN (Book #3)
IF SHE HID (Book #4)
IF SHE FLED (Book #5)
IF SHE FEARED (Book #6)
IF SHE HEARD (Book #7)

THE MAKING OF RILEY PAIGE SERIES
WATCHING (Book #1)
WAITING (Book #2)
LURING (Book #3)
TAKING (Book #4)
STALKING (Book #5)
KILLING (Book #6)

RILEY PAIGE MYSTERY SERIES
ONCE GONE (Book #1)
ONCE TAKEN (Book #2)
ONCE CRAVED (Book #3)
ONCE LURED (Book #4)
ONCE HUNTED (Book #5)
ONCE PINED (Book #6)
ONCE FORSAKEN (Book #7)

ONCE COLD (Book #8)
ONCE STALKED (Book #9)
ONCE LOST (Book #10)
ONCE BURIED (Book #11)
ONCE BOUND (Book #12)
ONCE TRAPPED (Book #13)
ONCE DORMANT (Book #14)
ONCE SHUNNED (Book #15)
ONCE MISSED (Book #16)
ONCE CHOSEN (Book #17)

MACKENZIE WHITE MYSTERY SERIES
BEFORE HE KILLS (Book #1)
BEFORE HE SEES (Book #2)
BEFORE HE COVETS (Book #3)
BEFORE HE TAKES (Book #4)
BEFORE HE NEEDS (Book #5)
BEFORE HE FEELS (Book #6)
BEFORE HE SINS (Book #7)
BEFORE HE HUNTS (Book #8)
BEFORE HE PREYS (Book #9)
BEFORE HE LONGS (Book #10)
BEFORE HE LAPSES (Book #11)
BEFORE HE ENVIES (Book #12)
BEFORE HE STALKS (Book #13)
BEFORE HE HARMS (Book #14)

AVERY BLACK MYSTERY SERIES
CAUSE TO KILL (Book #1)
CAUSE TO RUN (Book #2)
CAUSE TO HIDE (Book #3)
CAUSE TO FEAR (Book #4)
CAUSE TO SAVE (Book #5)
CAUSE TO DREAD (Book #6)

KERI LOCKE MYSTERY SERIES
A TRACE OF DEATH (Book #1)
A TRACE OF MURDER (Book #2)
A TRACE OF VICE (Book #3)
A TRACE OF CRIME (Book #4)

A TRACE OF HOPE (Book #5)

Made in United States
Troutdale, OR
06/18/2025